A Vineyard Lullaby

The Vineyard Sunset Series

Katie Winters

Chapter One

Much like her grandmother, Anna, who'd died long before her birth, Audrey Sheridan had always kept a diary. There had always been something about the process of it: putting pen to paper and building the story of your life, page after page. She always found unique poetry in her mistakes and her joys and her fears, something beautiful in the passage of time. Audrey Sheridan was only six weeks or so from her twentieth birthday, and her nineteenth year had been a real doozy. In the words of her Aunt Christine, "You did more living at age nineteen than most people get in before thirty." Her diary was proof of that— something that would be around after Audrey's death.

There was something about being pregnant, on the verge of giving birth to her very first child that made Audrey think a lot more about her legacy, about life cycles, about what would be remembered of her after she was gone. This was something Audrey had tried to describe to a friend at Penn State. The explanation had failed. Audrey no longer had the dialogue for a "college conversation." A frat party seemed like something from

1

an alien universe. Now, she knew only pregnancy, horrible aches and pains, heartburn, and deep fears that kept her awake all night long sometimes.

It was a gray morning at the end of February. The sun hardly bothered to lift its weary head across the Vineyard horizon, and the house was cast in a ghoulish light. Audrey sat delicately at the kitchen table and gazed over the Vineyard Sound waters. Since her arrival to Martha's Vineyard the previous summer, she'd hardly grown accustomed to the view. And in fact, the view seemed strangely different every day; a different boat graced the far-out waters, a bright cardinal flocked to the tree line, or snowstorms churned flakes across the yard and the dock. The seasons shifted around the big house, and all the while, her stomach had just grown bigger and bigger.

Audrey finished her journal entry for the morning and then flipped back to some of the first pages in the diary. She had started the thing at the end of May the previous year, as she'd headed off for her internship in Chicago. It was funny to read these entries.

May 28,

I know I'm on the right path. I was always meant to do journalism, ever since I forced Mom to do those mock interviews at our little crummy apartment in Boston. Our boss for the internship seems to like my stuff so far. I feel competitive with the other interns and already working my way up to write alongside some of the others in the office— people who have already graduated and begun their real careers.

Audrey clucked her tongue at the words. She half-remembered writing them. With every notation, she'd sizzled with adrenaline for the approaching weeks. She'd had her eye on the man who would eventually get her pregnant; she'd ached for him— not just because he'd been the most attractive man at the newspaper, but because he was incredibly brilliant, had won plenty of awards in journalism, and was the kind of person she wanted to latch onto if only to learn more about the journalistic world-at-large.

Now, she sat in the soft gray of her grandfather's house, just a little over thirty-eight weeks pregnant. She felt like a human bowling ball.

Funny what life did to you.

Suddenly, one of the bedroom doors off to her left pushed open. Amanda stood in an oversized t-shirt, her long locks wildly mussed as they curled down her shoulders. She blinked at Audrey with surprise as her lips stretched into a big yawn.

Finally, she collected herself enough to ask, "Couldn't sleep again?"

Audrey closed her diary quickly and arched an eyebrow toward her slightly-older cousin. "You know I don't need sleep. It's for the elderly, not young ones like us."

"Right," Amanda said with a slight roll of her eyes. She walked past the table and then eased into the kitchen area, pouring coffee into a filter, filling up the machine, and pressing the on-button. Her motions were zombic like. "Are you ready for the big day?"

Audrey splayed her hands across her belly. "It's a lot different than the parties I'm used to. But I guess if there's enough cake, I'll find a way not to complain."

Amanda chuckled. "I tried to see if we could get kegs filled with green juice, just so you'd feel more comfortable, but the keg hasn't moved on from beer, I guess."

"Thanks, cuz. Appreciate the effort," Audrey shot back.

Today was Audrey's baby shower. The date had been on the calendar for quite a while, but Audrey had always seen it so far off on the calendar. Now that it was here, it meant that the other stuff would come much too soon— labor, delivery. A real, three-dimensional human baby. It freaked her out.

Amanda sat across from Audrey at the kitchen table, blocking Audrey's view of the glowing sea. She sipped her coffee and went over her traditional to-do list, which she'd written up the previous night. Audrey teased Amanda about the "list thing" quite a bit. Although the girls were thick as thieves, very best friends in many respects, they were entirely different, with Audrey a traditional Type B (or Type C, really), and Amanda firmly rooted in her Type A nature.

That said, ever since Chris had left her at the altar and Amanda's life had gone off the rails, Amanda had loosened up quite a bit. It had been strange to watch as Amanda's room-mate, cousin, and dear friend. Sometimes, Audrey felt that she hadn't given enough moral support to Amanda since her permanent arrival in mid-January. But in other ways, she and Amanda had learned that sometimes, just sitting in silence was all that was needed. Neither of them wanted to feel alone.

"Okay. It looks like everyone will arrive at around one," Amanda said. "Your mom should be here soon to help me decorate this place and set up the games."

"Games?" Audrey scoffed.

"Yes, Aud. Games."

"Like pin the diaper on the baby?"

Amanda's cheeks brightened to crimson. "I mean, if you don't want to play that ..."

"No, no." Audrey's laughter made the baby thump a foot against the inside of her stomach. "We can play pin the diaper on the baby if you want. I mean, I know that's your favorite game."

"You don't have to be snarky one hundred percent of the day, Aud," Amanda returned.

"But then, how would I teach my daughter how to banter?" Audrey replied quickly, wearing the slightest smile on her lips.

"Your daughter is picking up on every little thing you say," Amanda said.

"Good. She'll come into the world a bossy little thing. Nobody will ever push her around."

* * *

At twelve-thirty, Audrey sat in the living room while her mother, Lola, Aunt Christine, Aunt Susan, and Amanda finalized the last elements of the baby shower decor. The speaker system played a song by Cher, which Audrey's mother hummed a bit too loudly as she carried a platter of baby-themed cookies— tiny shoes in pink and white— from the kitchen to the large table they had set up, closer to Audrey's chair. Audrey could see it in her mother's posture: Lola Sheridan was nervous. Not about the baby shower, exactly, but about all the chaos that would come afterward. She was going to be a grandmother. But stranger than that, her sister, Christine, planned to raise the baby for the first few years so Audrey could return to college and get that journalism degree she craved.

Audrey's mother hadn't taken so kindly to the idea the previous summer when Audrey and Christine had concocted it. Unfortunately for Lola, it wasn't her decision. It was Audrey's. Audrey, who'd had to grow up in a flash.

There was a rap on the door. Susan leaped toward the mudroom to open it. Bright voices swirled back through the hallway.

"Jennifer! It is so kind of you to drop this off yourself," Susan said.

"Don't worry about it. I was on my way to meet my son for a hike, anyway."

"A hike? In this weather? You're crazy," Susan said as she led Jennifer Conrad of the Frosted Delights Bakery in from the chill and toward the baby shower table.

Jennifer carried a glowing white box. When she stationed it on the table, she slowly eased the top off to reveal a five-tiered cake covered with beautiful pink roses and little golden jewels. It was a cake fit for a princess. Audrey had her eye on eating an entire tier to herself.

"Ta-da!" Jennifer said. She beamed down at Audrey. "What do you think? I know it's nothing compared to what your world-famous pastry-chef Aunt Christine can do, but it's some of my best work, if I say so myself. My mother helped me through a lot of the more complicated steps. And my boyfriend tried to eat a lot of the frosting before I had a chance to put it on the cake, but I managed to fight him off."

Audrey grinned up at the beautiful red-haired woman, whom she'd met briefly and heard so much about. Her mother had only just had a horrible stroke. She and her high school sweetheart had gotten divorced after many years of marriage—yet she seemed just as bright and chipper as ever. How did women in their forties do it? Audrey felt overwrought with emotion, sometimes, and struggled to see her way out of it.

There was something about women on the Vineyard. They pressed forward, no matter what the circumstances were.

"It's really beautiful," Audrey finally stated. "I just love it."

"Seriously. It's wonderful," Lola affirmed. "I'm so glad you said you'd take over. Christine has said all this time she could manage it, but we all knew the truth."

Christine flashed a big wave of dark hair over her shoulder. "Zach and I have been up to our ears arranging a nursery for the baby and a room for Audrey to have whenever she wants it. It's a lot more work than we thought."

"It always is," Jennifer said. "The nesting phase in pregnancy is always the most enjoyable time. But then again, so is the baby shower. Actually, it's all wonderful. And scary. And amazing."

Christine and Audrey locked eyes. They seemed to reflect the same thing. And in truth, all their conversations over the previous few weeks had revolved around the same topics of fear, excitement, and, ultimately, logistics. How would they make this work, exactly? Audrey was the mother and would always be. But Christine was a stand-in, prepared to take on the role of "mother" until Audrey was ready to do it full-time. This was to be her first shot at motherhood, a kind of practice round until Christine and Zach set about adopting a baby for their own family. She'd had to have an ovary removed many years ago; this was her only real option.

After Jennifer left, other guests began to file into the Sheridan house. Grandpa Wes, who'd headed back into his room for an afternoon nap, soon drew open his door to greet his family members and dear friends from across the island. He, too, locked eyes with Audrey across the growing crowd, but Audrey saw nothing but love and excitement reflected back. In some ways, Grandpa Wes was one of her dearest friends, even if he was her grandfather. She'd certainly spent more time with him over the previous eight months than she had with nearly anyone else. They were both always home together, and their bond had grown into something that Audrey couldn't even explain if she tried. She loved her grandfather more than life.

Sometimes, but only sometimes, Audrey had questioned this. What kind of nineteen-year-old girl's best friend was her grandfather with dementia?

Oh, but the friendship was something she wouldn't have traded for the world.

More people came with beautifully wrapped packages, bright smiles, and plenty of baked goods. There was Aunt Claire and Aunt Charlotte, along with Gail and Abby and Rachel, who stuck together, teenage best friends. Audrey chuckled inwardly that these girls, at fourteen and fifteen, were much closer in age to her than basically anyone else there. But she was the pregnant one, and therefore, she was deemed an "adult."

At least Audrey could act as an "always have safe sex!" lesson for the three of them.

Then, there was Aunt Kerry and Uncle Andy's new girl-friend, who Audrey had taken a liking to— Beth, who also brought her beautiful son, Will, who was on the spectrum. There was Aunt Kelli, along with Uncle Steven's wife, Laura. Even Natalie from the Sunrise Cove Inn came since Susan had recently hired that new young man to take on many of the responsibilities. Sam. He was so incredibly handsome, and it was clear to most that he was into Amanda.

In the wake of his employment at the inn, Audrey had poked and prodded Amanda for the details of their budding friendship. So far, Amanda had said they were "just friends," and "they were just there for each other." Audrey had bets they were well on their way toward a summertime romance.

The cake was starting to get eaten; conversation bubbled throughout the room; and every single woman came up to Audrey and Christine. They spoke about how "brave" they were and how "lovely" it was that they could build this "unique" relationship between themselves and the daughter growing in Audrey's stomach. Audrey's cheeks grew tired after multiple exclamations of, "That's so sweet of you!" and "Wow, you shouldn't have!" The smile-fatigue grew even worse as she opened her presents and thanked even more of her guests. She had grown accustomed to mid-day naps (like Grandpa Wes) and couldn't wait for everyone to duck out and leave her in peace.

Still, it was nice that so many people loved her.

Several guests had brought gender-neutral gifts for the baby, which Audrey scoffed at. In truth, she knew, beyond a shadow of a doubt, that her baby would be a girl. She simply didn't have it in her to deliver a boy. It was something Zach had teased her about over the past eight months, but she would hear nothing of it. The Sheridan girls would welcome as many girls into the fold as possible. Her mother and Aunt Susan had insisted she was carrying high, which meant a girl, so the deal was sealed in their minds. Maybe it was just a silly myth, but people truly believed in it. Either way, Audrey would be happy as long as she could count out ten toes and ten figures.

Toward the end of the baby shower, she opened a final gift from Aunt Kerry. In it, she found a bright pink, crocheted blanket, which she lifted to her cheek to rub the soft cotton against her skin.

"It's so beautiful, Aunt Kerry," she told the older woman in a soft murmur. "I know she'll love it so much."

Aunt Kerry reached her elderly hand across the space between them and patted Audrey on the thigh. Her eyes glowed as though they clung to tears.

"I hope you know we're so proud of you, Audrey," Aunt Kerry remarked with a soft smile.

Sometimes, Audrey took issue with this idea, that they were "proud" of her. After all, hadn't she just gotten herself knocked up in a faraway city by a stranger?

But she just nodded, smiled, and tried to keep her tears at bay. "Thank you, I love it so much, Aunt Kerry. And pink! It's already her favorite color."

"I figured," Aunt Kerry replied with a mischievous wink.

Chapter Two

Christine stood off toward the far end of the baby shower with her arms crossed anxiously over her chest. She knew Audrey well enough to sense how tired the poor girl was. She had yet another present propped up on her lap, and she stitched her eyebrows together as she nodded at something Kelli said about a favorite brand of spit-up towels when she'd been a young mother.

"That's good to know," Audrey said. "Thank you." There was just the tiniest strain to her voice, proof that she wanted a nap far more than any brand of spit-up towel.

But the Sheridan and Montgomery clan, along with other women from Oak Bluffs and beyond, were chatty, hungry, and eager. The party wouldn't close out anytime soon. There was too much food to eat, wine to drink, and gossip to fling around, which brought grateful gasps from all the visitors.

The door slammed from the driveway side of the house. Zach's voice hollered out as he entered, and Christine's heart jumped into her throat with excitement. Zach had closed the Bistro the previous night, opened it that morning, and said he would pop by the baby shower as soon as possible. Here he came, still dressed in his chef whites and with a smile filled with confidence. He beamed at all the Sheridan and Montgomery women and then stepped over to kiss Christine directly on the lips. Love was etched across both of their faces.

He was her partner in all things. The feelings she had for him pushed beyond all logic. When their kiss broke, his eyes held hers for a soft moment as he whispered, "I hope you know that cake I see over there can't compare with the one you would have made."

Christine giggled. "You know what to say to butter me up, don't you?"

"It's the truth," Zach replied. He stepped back, slung an arm over Christine's shoulder, and assessed the damage. "Audrey. It looks like you raked in the goods this afternoon."

Audrey cast him a mischievous glance. "We've got a lot to work with to help this baby girl grow up in the world."

"Right. A new Sheridan girl," Zach teased again. "You're just so sure of yourself."

"You know us Sheridan girls have a good dose of intuition, Zach," Lola said from the corner, beneath a heap of crumpled-up wrapping paper. "Have we ever been wrong about anything?"

"I know better than to second-guess any of you," Zach said. He grabbed a pretzel from a big serving bowl and took a small bite.

"And now you're going to help raise another Sheridan girl, so you'd better watch yourself," Susan told him from her stance near the kitchen entrance. "She'll have your heart the minute you look at her. And there's no turning back after that. That I can promise."

That moment, the back door slammed again. Two unfamiliar, very young-looking girls entered the living area. Initially, their bored-looking eyes grew wider, strange, as they spotted the enormous family before them. But a split-second later, they cried in unison, "Aud!" and burst toward the enormously pregnant woman, who they showered with hugs and kisses.

"You guys!" Audrey beamed. Her voice broke with emotion. "I had no idea you would come."

"We just didn't get the right ferry," one of the girls explained. "We had the time wrong."

"And then we had to hang out in godforsaken Falmouth for like, what, hours?" the other said.

"And we nearly froze to death."

"But it was all so we could see you before you pop!"

"You look great, Audrey. Big, but hot. You know, in a pregnant way."

The others at the baby shower turned from the wild teenage conversation to have words of their own— gossip about Oak Bluffs, people in Edgartown, and one another. Audrey slowly drew to her feet and hobbled toward the kitchen table, where she gestured toward her two beautiful friends and said, "Aunt Christine! I want you to meet my best friends from college. Cassie and Willa. I can't believe they came all this way."

Christine shook their hands. "I think it's a good chance you made Audrey's day today, girls."

"We just can't wait to have her back at Penn State," Willa affirmed. "When she told us she was pregnant, we were like, bye-bye forever, Audrey!"

"But you're going to raise the baby while she finishes her degree?" Cassie asked.

Christine's heart pumped strangely in her chest. Again, she and Audrey made heavy eye contact. Christine acknowledged her fear surrounding this arrangement. Once the baby girl was born, would Audrey allow this to happen? Could she really leave the baby Christine already had her dreams set on?

"Seems like it," Christine said. She forced her voice to brighten and wore a small smile.

"Which means you're the adoptive dad of the year," Willa said to Zach slightly flirtatiously.

Zach chuckled and gripped Christine's waist a bit harder—proof he was with her till the end. "I don't know about that. But I'll be there for all the messy bits. That's for sure."

* * *

The party carried on for many hours. Audrey's college friends perked her up a great deal and managed to yank her over to a far corner to fill her head with gossip from the campus and get her all revved up for the following semester, when she would make her "big return."

Zach splayed a plate of cake onto Christine's flat palm and nodded. "You really should try it. I know you're averse to all other cakes besides your own, but the Frosted Delights is nothing to scoff at."

"You know I don't scoff at their stuff," Christine said. "Their donuts got me through December." In truth, she just had very little appetite, with the baby's due date fast approaching. She would be there within the month.

In the corner, Willa and Cassie got into a little tuff about the baby's birth date.

"She should really come now," Willa said. "Don't you want a little Pisces baby, Audrey? A little girl who's so sensitive and sweet?"

"No. She wants an Aries baby," Cassie affirmed. "You want a girl who will take life by the horns. Like you, Aud. You're a classic Aries baby."

"Don't I know she is," Lola chimed in as she stepped past them, whipping her long hair out behind her. "Audrey never listened to reason as a kid. She was all passion. Classic Aries."

"Classic Aries," both Cassie and Willa echoed back.

Christine placed the tongs of her fork into the cake and drew back the tiniest bite. As she chewed, she glanced back up at Zach, whose gaze turned toward the Vineyard Sound. She had grown accustomed to that look. There was something on his mind, something he needed to hash out. Slowly, she placed her half-eaten cake on the side table, rose, and slipped her fingers through his.

"Why don't we take a little walk? I could use some fresh air," she whispered in his ear.

They bundled up against the late-February chill and stepped out. Their boots made soft crunches through the snow as they eased around the house and out toward the last light over the Vineyard Sound. It seemed strange that in just a few weeks, spring would unravel this hard winter, melt the snow, and draw up mud from the depths below. Winter seemed to have its grip on everything.

When they reached the dock, Zach drew his thick arm around her and tugged her close to him. They gazed out across the waters, not saying a word but just enjoying the view. Christine's mind felt heavy with summertime memories, times when they'd eased out across the waves in just their swimsuits and felt the glorious browning of their skin beneath the sun.

"I've thought about her so much over the past few weeks," Zach said.

Christine shifted just the slightest bit. Through all this, she'd guessed that Zach's first child, the daughter who had died, had consumed a large part of his mind. He'd hardly spoken about her since he'd fessed up the story the previous summer.

Now, it practically felt as though the girl was right there with them.

"It must feel so complicated," Christine whispered, tilting her head to look at Zach.

"I have to say. It makes me really remember how much I

loved her— how she was on my mind every morning, every evening, and every split second in between. She still is, in a way, but it's different now. The worst thing in the world happened to her. So it's not like I can take care of her anymore," Zach resigned.

Christine felt the words like a punch to the stomach. For the first time in a long time, she thought back to when she had first known Zach all the way back in high school. They'd hated each other, despite their lust for one another. But beyond that, they'd been so innocent, hadn't they? Anna Sheridan had still been alive. Zach hadn't known the depths of loss yet. They'd been fresh-faced and ready to take on the world, living like they were untouchable in so many ways.

It made sense that they were a bit guarded now. They were older, courageous, but not stupid. Maybe that could be their motto as parents.

"I still want all of that with you, Christine," Zach said softly. "This baby and then more, if we can manage it. I've been reading so much on adoption websites lately. These kids have lost their parents, or their parents never wanted them in the first place. They're lost children in the world just looking for someone to love them. And I kind of see us as lost, too. In our special kind of way."

Christine dropped her head onto his chest. She tried to blink back tears, but they ran heavily down her cheeks. She'd never felt such incredible hope.

"I love you so much, Zach. You've already been a wonderful father. I am so glad you can do it all over again," Christine breathed. "You deserve it."

When they returned to the house, several of the guests had already left the party. Christine caught Cassie opening a bottle of wine, and instead of reprimanding the girl (who was probably only twenty), she just stuck out her wine glass and asked for a pour. In just a half-hour, Christine, Susan, Audrey,

Amanda, Cassie, Willa, and Lola sat around the kitchen table as Zach drove back to their house, and Wes returned to his bedroom for an early night.

"I think it's time we had another serving of cake," Lola announced with a sneaky grin. "Jennifer baked us enough to feed a small country."

The cake was portioned out, and more wine was poured. Conversation sprung up, lively and noisy, with Lola describing a recent article she'd written for *The New York Times* and Susan and Amanda speaking excitedly about a recent case they had decided to take on at their law office.

Only Audrey seemed serene, soft, quiet— words that didn't normally describe her. Without the others noticing, Christine reached over and squeezed Audrey's shoulder until Audrey's beautiful eyes turned toward hers.

With their eyes locked, Christine mouthed the words, "We got this. You know that?"

Audrey nodded back. "We got this."

Chapter Three

Audrey hovered by the back door and watched as Cassie and Willa pushed their feet into their designer boots and drew their winter coats over their small, girlish shoulders. Once upon a time, they'd been the Three Musketeers of their dorm hall, "girls who drank together, who stayed together," and, beyond one incident, during which Audrey had kissed a boy who Cassie had had a crush on—they'd avoided most typical freshman-year arguments.

In the wake of her pregnancy, Audrey had had to opt out of the apartment she had planned to share with the two of them, which had led them to add another girl to their roster. The girl was, apparently, "just fine," but maybe a bit too into studying. "She doesn't even go out on Thursdays," Cassie informed Audrey. "It's so lame."

"Thank you girls so much for coming," Audrey said as she studied their faces. "Are you sure you don't want to spend the night?"

"My mom booked us a little hotel room for the night,"

Cassie explained. "And then we have to take the first ferry back. I have a huge test Monday."

"And I have a date tomorrow!" Willa stated.

Audrey's heart swelled with envy. What would she give to just go on a simple date with a handsome college guy? What would she give to just make out with a stranger? Nobody would touch her with a five-foot pole, not now that she looked like a round monster.

"Good luck," Audrey said as she gave each a final hug. "I'll miss you every single day."

Audrey returned to the living room to find Aunt Susan in the first stages of cleaning up. This was her Aunt Susan, the first to leap on the tasks that needed to be done. Behind her, Amanda followed suit. She placed several paper plates into a plastic trash bag and gave Audrey a sleepy smile.

"Your friends are so cute," she said.

Audrey wondered if Amanda said this because she thought Cassie and Willa were slightly "immature" compared to Amanda's law school friends.

But she soon shook the thought out of her head. She was pregnant and over-stuffed and uncomfortable and nervous. Her emotions were all over the board, and she felt much more sensitive than she normally did. Amanda had meant no harm. She knew it was just her hormones out of whack.

"I'm so glad they came," Audrey said softly. "It had been way too long."

"Did they say they already picked an apartment for next semester?" Lola asked as she scrubbed the top of the table.

"They did, actually," Audrey replied. Why was it her voice still sounded so far away? "They told me the third room is mine if I want it."

"Perfect," Lola said. Her smile seemed hesitant, as though she wanted to say a whole lot more than that.

But Audrey cut everyone off. She turned toward the staircase, gripped the railing, and said, "I am so exhausted. I feel like I've run a marathon."

"You should get some rest, pumpkin," Aunt Susan told her as she furrowed her brow. "I think we had a pretty successful party. Thanks for playing along."

The words rang through Audrey's head as she slipped herself into bed and stared at the darkness above. Her fingers drummed across her chest. When her stomach had first started to grow, she had laughed at the way her blankets had followed outward as well. Now she was a big ball of baby, and it didn't make her laugh any longer.

Usually, when she lay back like this at night, her thoughts turned to the future, of when she might meet someone else, a guy she might want to do this whole baby-thing with properly. She imagined him, late at night, with his head propped up on her stomach. She imagined him saying, *"I can hear her. I know what she said."* The face of this mystery man was blank, but his voice was deep, assured. Audrey fell in love with him, despite the fact that he didn't even exist.

She supposed all this love that ballooned in her was due to the baby. The extra love came with the pregnancy like a toy came with a Happy Meal. She wasn't sure what she would do with all this "extra love" when she returned to the Penn State campus in the fall. She hoped her body would be back to "normal" by then, but that seemed wildly improbable.

However, her mother, Lola Sheridan, had bounced back almost immediately after giving birth to Audrey. So maybe it wasn't completely wild to hope.

* * *

Several hours later, Audrey's eyes burst open as she felt her stomach tighten into a painful crap. It radiated from the top, wrapped around her belly, and then ran down her back. It was a deep-rooted cramp, one that made her squeeze her toes tightly and stab her palms with her fingernails. The pain was small, and then it grew tremendous. It was as though a wave washed over and swallowed her whole. It reminded Audrey of a previous time when she'd been out to dinner with Susan, her mother, Christine, and Amanda— and she'd nearly fainted with the pain in the coatroom at the Sunrise Cove Inn.

That had been false labor pain. Assuredly, this was, too. After it subsided, Audrey took a deep breath and leaned against the headboard. She sat there rubbing her belly for about five minutes before she felt another one start. She concentrated as she shut her eyes tight, willing the pain to go away, but it shot through her spine and then splintered across her belly like fireworks. During the contraction, her belly tightened into a ball.

What. The. Heck.

After several minutes of pain, Audrey placed her feet on the floor at the side of her bed and flicked on the lamp. His phone read 2:43. It was too early for anything.

Gingerly, she stepped out into the hallway and walked slowly down the staircase. Once down there, another contraction shot through her all over again, and she nearly fell to the ground but grabbed the counter in time. All the color drained from her cheeks. She'd planned to sit at the kitchen table, write in her diary, or maybe watch a little TV. With each passing moment, it was obvious that she had to do something about this.

But there was no way that baby Sheridan was ready to greet them. It was still about two weeks too early. And two weeks felt like an enormous amount of time to Audrey— enough time to get her head around her baby's birth.

Besides, if she was honest with herself, she wanted an Aries baby— one like herself.

About fifteen minutes later, Audrey concluded that this pain wasn't going anywhere. Initially, she texted Amanda for help but knew that her only real option was to knock on Amanda's door. They were the only ones home, as Susan had run off to Scott's, Christine was with Zach, and Audrey's mother was off in her cabin in the woods with Tommy.

It was just the grandkids and Grandpa Wes and a potential labor that was now brewing full force...fun.

Amanda's meek voice came out of the darkness. "Come in," she murmured as Audrey creaked the door open. Amanda's eyes squeezed shut as the soft light poured over them. "What's up, babe?"

Audrey stood in the doorway as another crashing wave came over her. She placed her hand on her stomach and suddenly, without pause she burst into tears and started panicking. Immediately, Amanda leaped from her bed, turned on the lamp, and blinked big eyes at Audrey.

"What's wrong, honey?" she asked. She gripped Audrey's hand, closed the door, and led her to the edge of her bed.

Fat tears rolled down Audrey's cheeks. She'd never felt so outside of time. Her thoughts were scattered. She only heard every few of Amanda's words.

"It hurts so much," Audrey finally stuttered. Then she sucked in a breath to try to calm herself. She stirred with anxiety and then slowly fell back onto Amanda's pillow. She thought she might vomit but bit hard on her lower lip.

"You still have two weeks to go," Amanda said softly. "Maybe it's just a false alarm, like last time?"

"I hope so," Audrey said. "I ate way too much cake at the party. Maybe it triggered her."

Amanda laughed warmly and adjusted herself alongside Audrey. She gripped her hand, which Audrey immediately squeezed as hard as she could due to fear, pain, and everything in between.

"Ouch," Amanda whispered as Audrey let her grip loosen.

"Sorry," Audrey said, although she truly didn't mean it.

A few times, Amanda tried to start up some kind of conversation with Audrey— about her college friends, about the year ahead, or even about what one of the Kardashians had done recently. But each time, the words buzzed through Audrey's ears and seemed nonsensical. It was like Amanda and Audrey were deep underwater yet still trying their best to have a conversation.

At just past four in the morning, Audrey cried in alarm and nearly broke Amanda's finger bones. Amanda coaxed Audrey to take deep breaths, breathing in and out to try to calm her. When the contraction stopped, Amanda removed her bright red and white fingers from Audrey's grip, jumped over Audrey's legs, and grabbed her phone. Through moans, Audrey asked her what she was doing.

"Hey! Mom? Sorry to wake you up. I think it's the real deal with Audrey. Yep. Heavy contractions every five to seven minutes now. I think I'm going to take her in. Could you call Aunt Lola and Aunt Christine? Great. Thank you."

Audrey clamped her eyes shut and pursed her lips in a straight line. Somewhere in the back alleys of her mind, she'd thought that maybe, if she'd tried hard enough or hid out here in Amanda's room, she would be able to stop the labor.

But it was clear: Baby Sheridan was headed straight toward them, like a rocket ship on the way to the moon.

Amanda was all movement after that. After all, she was Susan Sheridan's daughter, and she'd had a to-do list for Audrey's labor and delivery since about January 21, when she had decided to stick around a bit longer. Audrey had also teased her about this incessantly. Right now, though, she was grateful for it.

"I also already packed you a bag," Amanda said as she yanked open the closet and grabbed one for her and one for Audrey. "I have all the essentials in there. And I even researched what most mothers wish they would have brought once they're at the hospital."

"I don't know what I would do without you," Audrey told her. Her voice hummed with her familiar sarcasm, but both Amanda and Audrey knew how much she meant it.

"Okay. I have to wake up Grandpa," Amanda said as she shoved a sweatshirt over her head and ruffled her hair.

Amanda disappeared for a few minutes, while Audrey fell into another wave of panic, pain, and horror. She heard the vague grunts of her Grandpa Wes, who was very confused. She then heard Amanda's explanation, which was met with excitement and fear and a number of "Wow!"s from her grandfather. Despite the pain, even Audrey had to grin. He was so exuberant.

She supposed it made sense, as he hadn't been allowed the beauty of a family, closeness, and love in many years. He was the most selfless man she knew in the world. How grateful she was for him.

And, of course, her gratitude was only compounded a few minutes later, as she sat tenderly in the car's back seat with Grandpa Wes himself. He beamed at her, excited, then splayed out his hand and bowed his head toward it.

"You can try to break my fingers if you want to," he told her with a sly grin. "Your grandmother very nearly did when she went into labor with Susan. I'll never forget it. My fingers certainly haven't."

Wordless, Audrey slipped her hand through her grandfather's fingers and dropped her head back against the car seat headrest. Amanda started the engine and slowly eased them through the snowy, somber, dark morning. Audrey's stomach and back continued to roar with ever-present pain as each contraction became stronger and stronger. All the while, she squeezed her grandfather's hand until she felt sure she might break the bones.

Grandpa Wes didn't complain.

Not even once.

Chapter Four

During Audrey's first semester at Penn State, she had told some of her new friends she was clairvoyant. *"I swear. Think something, anything, and I will tell you what you're thinking,"* she'd said between vodka shots. *"I swear. I'll know."*

As Audrey lay back in the hospital bed as the clock rounded over into five in the morning, she remembered this long-ago era and felt, with a funny twitch in the back of her mind, that she could read exactly what her mother was thinking. Lola hovered to the left of the hospital bed; her eyes were large, and they reflected excitement and fear for Audrey. She gazed down at her one and only daughter. All the color drained from her cheeks while she tried to smile.

"Stop looking at me like that," Audrey finally gasped. She scrunched her forehead and blinked up at her mother. "You're looking at me like you think I'm going to— "

She couldn't finish the sentiment. It was too dark. And Christine interrupted her, anyway.

"Those contractions were closer, weren't they?" she asked.

Audrey nodded in response as the fear consumed her. She was sure her mother could see it clearly etched on her face and in her eyes now. Lola grabbed her daughter's hand, knowing she was frightened, and squeezed it gently. "You got this, okay? You're going to be fine, honey. You're a Sheridan. You got this!"

In all honesty, she was terrified but so grateful to have her mother by her side. The baby was too early, and the nurses seemed rushed and panicked. They had hooked up a Doppler device to monitor the baby's heart rate, and every time they looked at the monitor, a weird look marred their faces. This was no "typical" birth. Audrey sensed it, but she couldn't fully prepare for it. All they kept telling her was to breathe and push through the contractions when they came like she was taught in Lamaze classes. She wished it was that simple.

Audrey finally looked at the nurse who was jotting down something on her chart and asked, "Is everything okay?" The nurse turned and placed a hand on her belly. "Everything is fine, honey. This is standard procedure, and you have nothing to worry about." She flashed Audrey a smile before leaving the room.

Time operated strangely. There was a lot of downtime. Audrey dropped her head back on the pillow, billowed out her cheeks, and watched videos on her phone for a while. Her Aunt Christine and her mother seemed busy texting. Probably, they texted one another, as they didn't want to worry Audrey.

"Hey," Audrey said at around nine in the morning.

This forced both of their eyes upward. They looked like frightened children who'd been caught in the middle of doing something wrong. Audrey giggled softly, then shrugged and said, "Don't worry about it. Get back to your text marathon."

Lola popped up from the chair again, walked toward Audrey, and smoothed her hair behind her ear. "You okay, honey?"

Audrey shrugged. "I guess. Just waiting for another round of pain, you know? That's all life is."

Lola rolled her eyes and turned back toward Christine. "Did you just hear what my nineteen-year-old daughter told me?"

Christine chuckled. "She sounds like she knows what she's talking about."

"You're not even twenty years old!" her mother said with a wry smile.

"We can talk the optimism back into her after labor and delivery," Christine stated as she stood up from her chair. "Right now, Audrey, you can be just as sarcastic and pessimistic as you want to be."

"I just want to make sure my baby's first words are sarcastic," Audrey groaned, trying to get comfortable. "Christine, if I'm not around for a while, you have to put the phone up by her crib and let me talk to her. Every day, I need her to know and learn my unique snarkiness."

"Maybe she'll luck out and be more like Amanda. Or Susan," Lola replied with a hearty laugh. "Responsible and kind."

"That sounds awful," Audrey affirmed. "Don't tell Amanda I said that. You know I love her more than anything."

"Maybe your baby will come out with a to-do list all made-up," Christine teased. "Number one. Learn how to talk. Number two. Learn how to walk. Number three. Rule the world."

But again, another contraction rolled through Audrey's body. She scrunched her eyes tight as the muscles in her stomach hardened and knocked her head deeper into her pillow. The moan that escaped her lips didn't sound like her. It sounded animalistic. Audrey started to pant quickly now.

"Slow down your breathing, honey. You don't want to

hyperventilate," Lola told her while running a hand through her hair.

When the contraction finally ended, Audrey blinked through her tears and looked at her mother and Aunt Christine alongside her bed. They both looked like worried mother hens.

"Are you guys also in labor?" Audrey asked as her voice rasped. "You look like you're going through something."

Christine laughed and then excused herself a few minutes later to grab some food down the hall. This left mother, daughter, and incoming granddaughter there in the hospital room. Lola lifted Audrey's hand to her lips and kissed it tenderly. It had been quite a while since Audrey had been alone with her mother. In previous years, it had only been the two of them. Now, they had the entire Sheridan universe.

"Hi, Mom." Audrey's words were simple, yet they also embodied all these thoughts at once. "How are you hanging in there?"

Her mother's eyes glowed as she chuckled. "How am I doing? You know, I watched you the other night with your friends from college."

Audrey arched an eyebrow. "Creep."

Her mother chuckled. "No. Not like that. But I noticed something. I noticed how much more mature you are than them, now."

Audrey rolled her eyes playfully. "Really, Mom? Mature?"

"Seriously. I know you never wanted that word to be attributed to you, but here we are. Those girls are living out their college days, doing homework, and flirting with boys. And I know you want that life back so badly. But I can't help but admire the person you've grown into while you've been here on the Vineyard."

Aunt Christine entered the room again with two steaming cups of coffee. She glanced from Audrey to Lola and back again, as though she sensed the seriousness of the conversation.

She then passed the coffee off to Lola. Audrey's throat felt thick with sorrow and fear. She wanted to tell her mother not to say any more, not so soon before she gave birth to her daughter. It almost felt as though she was saying goodbye.

The pain ramped up, hour after hour. Before long, Audrey had been in labor for ten hours, and the fatigue, confusion, and fear swirled in the back of her mind like a kind of storm. When she blinked forward, she saw dark and white spots. The pain itself seemed to be the color red. Sometimes, it was separate from herself, something she was battling, and at other times, the pain seemed to extend along her entire body. She heard her primal screams erupt from her own throat only sometimes; other times, they seemed to come from some other place.

The real games began at about eleven o'clock at night— around nineteen hours after Audrey's arrival at the hospital. All eyes were upon her in the delivery room. She was propped up, with her legs in stirrups, and the space between her legs all on display for everyone to see.

Vaguely, she joked to Aunt Christine that she felt like some girl at a fraternity party— always ready to open her legs wide! At this, Lola said, "Audrey! That's an awful thing to say," even as Christine burst into wild laughter.

Obviously, emotions were high. In the midst of horrendous pain, Audrey didn't care who was looking at her privates. She just wanted everything to be okay and over with. She always wanted everything to be okay.

The pain was astronomical. Audrey glared at the doctor between her legs like he was the devil himself. He coaxed her, along with her mother and Aunt Christine, to "give all you got with this contraction," and "just another push," and "just another one."

"I can see the head," the doctor told her.

It seemed strange that this man should see her baby before

she ever did. Audrey craned forward to take a peek but couldn't yet see anything over the big mound of belly she still had.

"Come on. One final push," he told her.

"One more, Audrey!" her mother cried.

With a wild rush of adrenaline, Audrey shut her eyes, gritted her teeth and performed one final, horrible, wretched push.

And at that moment, her baby entered the world.

But after that, seconds blurred together strangely.

There was no cry from the baby. The limbs flailed a bit as the doctor snipped the umbilical cord and instructed a nurse to take the baby away. Audrey's eyes turned, panicked, toward her mother's. She knew at that moment that her mother had even less idea of what had happened than Audrey did. Her heart fell into the space in her belly where her baby had been.

"Where are you taking her?" Audrey demanded.

"Audrey, we still need to get the placenta out," the doctor informed her.

"Where are you taking her?" she asked again. This time, her voice sounded forceful and aggressive. She wanted to know what was happening.

"Your baby needs a little help," the doctor said. "And we need to get this placenta out of you. One more push for me, okay?"

Audrey's nostrils flared as she did his bidding. How she hated this man! Maybe she would have smacked him across the face if she'd been anywhere else but in this vulnerable spot. She had never felt this kind of panic before. As she pushed with another contraction, she let out a loud groan and then fell back against her bed, feeling exhausted. Tears rolled down her cheeks as she turned her attention toward her mother.

"Mom, where did they take her? What is going on?"

Lola squeezed Audrey's hand, which was pale. "I don't know. I don't know, baby."

"Find out!" Audrey demanded. Anger flew through her. "FIND OUT."

The news came shortly after, just as the doctor realized that Audrey was hemorrhaging.

"Your baby isn't breathing properly," the doctor informed her, even as the world began to cave in, and Audrey's blurry view grew even blurrier. "We had to put him on a breathing machine. We'll know more soon."

Aunt Christine and Audrey's mother's voices swirled together in a kind of haunting sing-song. Audrey blinked into nothingness and felt herself give over yet again to pain. She couldn't comprehend what the doctor was saying.

My baby isn't breathing. Am I hemorrhaging? My baby isn't breathing.

Several minutes or hours later, Audrey had no idea how to tell— she lifted her eyes to find her mother slumped over in her chair with her palm across her cheek and her eyes toward the floor. It was clear she had been crying. Audrey's heart hammered in her throat. She opened her lips to try to ask the question she so desperately needed the answer to—

But her throat and lips felt as though they'd never tasted water before.

Finally, she heard herself whisper, "Mom? Mommy?"

But somewhere, from the depths of whatever sleep Lola was in, she heard her daughter's voice. She jumped from the chair, rushed toward her, dropped down, and presented Audrey with the slightest smile. She passed her some water so she could take a drink.

"How are you doing, Audrey? Oh, my baby. You did amazing. You know that?"

Audrey's eyes filled again with tears. She feared the worst so much that, now, she dreaded to ask.

"They've taken your baby to the NICU," Lola finally explained, as though she could sense the ominous question hanging in the air. "You need to rest, Audrey. Your baby is in good hands, but you have lost a lot of blood. You need to rest. They've done all they can so far, and they will keep going. Trust them."

But Audrey couldn't possibly trust them. She placed a tired hand over her stomach and felt outraged with panic. This baby had been a part of her for almost nine months! She'd carried it with her everywhere! She'd felt they could dream the same dreams!

And now, what?

She just prayed that the medical team knew what they were doing.

She burst into another round of tears, ones that shook her entire frame. Finally, she gave herself over to sleep again, knowing that it awaited her, anyway. Her body was sore and uncomfortable. Once upon a time, maybe, Audrey had had control over that body.

She no longer felt she did.

Chapter Five

Christine didn't know she was shaking. She stood just outside the labor and delivery section of the hospital with her knees knocking together and her eyes glazed over. It was just past midnight, and she'd spent the previous twenty-some hours at the hospital. She spread a hand out against the nearest wall and attempted to steady herself. With each blink, she saw only the tormented face of Audrey as she'd gone through a very rough birth.

Now, the baby had been rushed away, and the doctors had said only, "We'll let you know when we know more." In essence, the baby wasn't breathing, Audrey was hemorrhaging, the world had stopped spinning, and Christine had forgotten why the heck she had come out into the hallway in the first place. She wanted to crumple up into a ball and give herself over to pain.

A hand wrapped around her shoulder. Suddenly, she whirled around and fell into the open, strong arms of Zach. She squeezed her eyes shut as a wail erupted from her throat. She hadn't seen Zach since hours before, when she'd checked on the rest of them in the waiting room, had a brief coffee, and told them, "Everything is going to plan— right on schedule."

When their hug broke, Zach dropped his nose against Christine's and gazed into her eyes. His own glowed with tears. He played with her hair and gently set it back across her shoulders.

"What happened?" he finally asked.

Christine hardly recognized his voice. For the first time since she had fallen in love with him, she could see the man he'd been in the wake of his daughter's death. She could see the real damage, the real heartache.

"I don't know. One minute we were telling her to push, and then the next thing we knew, the baby was whisked away in a panicked rush. They said the baby wasn't breathing. They told us to wait. And then, Audrey started to hemorrhage, and we were all told to leave the room. I just came out here. I just ... "

Christine gasped again as her tears took hold once more and she couldn't stand still. After a moment, she sucked in a breath and strung her fingers through Zach's, and the two of them walked out toward the coffee and vending machines located next to where the family sat, waiting in uncomfortable plastic chairs, their eyes downcast. Amanda hustled up, her eyes tinged with red. Susan appeared beside them a second later, as well.

"What happened? Are they okay?" Amanda rasped. The panic in her voice was clear as day.

"We're still waiting to hear," Christine murmured. Slowly, she lifted a quarter from her change purse and pushed it into the old coffee machine. She didn't have a second one, but Zach did, and he slipped that in after hers. They watched, stunned, as the coffee began to trickle into a little plastic cup. It felt so surreal that the world could end in such a way, and there could still be bad coffee made in machines at the hospital.

Christine explained to Amanda and Susan what had

happened. Amanda asked a whole host of questions, which proved that she'd done a lot more research about childbirth than probably Audrey even had. This was just her way.

"Can we see her yet?" Amanda demanded.

"I think they'll keep her here for a few days, but she really needs her rest," Christine said. "She was so strong in there."

Even as she said it, she could feel what she actually meant echoing back the words: *she was strong, but maybe not strong enough— maybe not strong enough.*

How awful.

Amanda turned toward her mother and placed her head heavily on Susan's shoulder. Susan bit hard on her lower lip as she comforted her daughter. If they all fell apart, they wouldn't be able to pick one another back up. Susan, as usual, had to be the strongest.

Lola appeared in the doorway of the waiting room a few minutes after that. Christine peered up at her from the top of her stale coffee. They'd been through war together, she and Lola and Audrey, and now, as she looked at Lola, she felt a strange kinship. Her eyes were even more bloodshot than Amanda's, and she staggered toward Christine with her arms outstretched. Christine wrapped her up and felt a guttural scream curve up from the base of Lola's belly and through her throat. She stifled it slightly in Christine's shoulder as Christine hung onto her. The pain was enormous.

A few minutes later, Lola took a few deep breaths, wiped her tears away, and finally let go of Christine. "Audrey is sleeping," Lola whispered. She dropped back in a chair and covered her eyes with the tops of her sleeves. "My baby is sleeping. And her baby, well. They want to talk to us in a little while, Christine. Can you come with me? Please?"

Christine had never heard her younger sister sound so meek before. Always, Lola had been the brash, powerful, wild one. Now, if a wind had cut through the hospital doors, she might have fallen to her knees.

About an hour later, Christine and Lola held hands as they walked through the glowing white hallways to meet with Audrey's doctor. Christine wanted to comment on how strange time was in a hospital. All the nurses, doctors, and patients operated like they had no idea it was around one in the morning. Everything was busy and excitable; nurses joked together at their nursing stations, and doctors ate their snacks where they could. There was no stopping sickness; there was no stopping deliveries; there was no stopping God's plan. Still, as Christine walked like a zombie toward this meeting, she wished she could press rewind and return to a long-ago day in the sun, with Audrey newly pregnant and just the possibility of all this stretched out before them.

Why hadn't they considered any of these turn of events? Were they too optimistic? Too idealistic? Too naïve?

One of the few times Susan had ever visited Christine in New York City, Christine had gotten one of her ovaries removed. It had been a time of horror and loneliness in her life. Her body had decided it no longer wanted to operate alongside her, but against her, and during the weeks before her procedure, she had drunk much more than she ever had before. She'd been so conscious of the escape. Every glass of wine poured meant a few minutes away from the reality that she would never be a mother on her own.

Now, she might never be a mother, period.

In the doctor's office, Lola and Christine continued to grip hands as they learned about the fate of Audrey's baby.

"As you know, the baby was not breathing immediately after delivery," the doctor started to explain. He folded his hands beneath his chin.

Christine wondered how many meetings he had to have

like this per day. How much bad news did he shell out in a week? Did he have a particular script he liked to use? Probably, they taught everyone that at medical school: how to let people down the easy way.

"We have him in the NICU to receive oxygen and for continual observation," the doctor continued. "And our diagnosis is Acute Respiratory Distress Syndrome."

Christine felt the words wrap around her throat and suffocate her. She turned her eyes toward Lola, who was just as pale as snow.

"What is that?" Lola whispered.

"Essentially, this occurs when fluid fills up the air sacs in the baby's lungs. When there's too much fluid in the lungs, there is either too little oxygen or too much carbon dioxide in the bloodstream."

Christine squeezed Lola's hand harder as her knees clacked together. A heavy silence fell over them. Christine could feel the tears stream down her cheeks.

"What happens now?" Christine finally asked, looking up at the doctor. "And is Audrey okay?"

The doctor nodded. "Audrey just needs to be monitored for a day or two. What happened with her hemorrhaging is quite common, and she's young, which means her body is strong and able to handle all this."

"And the baby?" Lola demanded. Her voice was edged with fear.

"ARDS normally gets worse before it gets better," the doctor said somberly. "The next three or four days will tell the tale. It will give us a lot more information about the next few weeks."

"Weeks?" Christine demanded.

The doctor didn't seem phased at all by Christine and Lola's panic. Again, Christine wanted to rip him to shreds and demand if he cared at all. This wasn't just another patient. This was Audrey's baby. This was Lola's grandbaby. This was the baby she had pledged to protect.

"What is the standard timeline for all this?" Lola finally whispered.

The doctor arched a salt and pepper eyebrow. "Normally, the disease gets worse for about three or four days. We have the baby connected to a nasal continuous positive airway pressure machine or NCPAP machine for short."

Christine wanted to tell him that she couldn't keep up with all this ridiculous lingo and to talk in lay terms, but she kept her lips sealed shut.

"And we will monitor his oxygen levels and carbon dioxide levels over the next few days before we plan out the next steps," the doctor said.

They both shook the doctor's hand and thanked him for all he had done so far before they headed back out into the hall-way. They continued to walk hand-in-hand, each dealing with their own waves of dread.

Lola and Christine stood outside Audrey's room several minutes later. Neither of them had been able to speak since they'd left the doctor's office. The diagnosis seemed like something that happened to other people, not to the Sheridan girls.

Maybe normally, had the circumstances been different, they might have said something like: *We can get through this. We can get through anything.*

But there was something much more sinister about this. About a baby they'd only just met being hooked up to a machine in the NICU.

Another silent minute passed and then another.

Suddenly, Lola blurted out, "Wait a minute. Did he say the baby was a he?"

Christine's heart thudded strangely. "No, he couldn't have."

Lola turned to her quickly and grabbed her forearm. "I'm pretty sure he did."

Christine furrowed her brow. This, too, felt like something from another dimension. Audrey had been so sure. They'd all been so sure.

But then again, they'd also been sure they'd have a safe birth. In another world, they were already back at the Sheridan house, with their new baby Sheridan girl fast asleep in her crib; in this reality, Audrey was asleep in her bed, and they were overstuffed with dessert and wine and love, all of them together, in the forever-warmth of that house.

"I'll go sit with her for a while," Lola finally said. She brought a strand of hair behind her ear.

For the first time ever, Lola Sheridan looked her age.

Christine had never seen that before.

"I'm going to go check on Zach," Christine said.

They hugged a final time before they parted ways. Just before Lola pressed her hand against the door, she turned and said, "Tell Tommy my phone is dead. I'll come out and say hello to him in a while, okay?"

Christine nodded and then walked off.

A few hours later, she and Zach found themselves in front of the glass at the NICU. Zach hadn't been very talkative, but both had agreed they wanted to say hello to the baby, a real hello before they left the hospital to get any kind of rest. They stood like ghosts in front of several very sick babies, all connected to machines. Toward the far right, a baby's crib read, "SHERIDAN," and beneath it, "UNNAMED, MALE."

Zach's voice cracked as he spoke for the first time in over an hour.

"Audrey is going to be so pissed."

Christine's heart burst into a million pieces. "Why?"

"Because she had a baby boy. All she ever wanted was a girl."

He tried to laugh at his joke. But the joke fell flat almost immediately, and his face contorted as he let out a horrible sob. All they'd really wanted, beyond anything, was a healthy baby. Nothing else had ever mattered.

Chapter Six

Zach and Christine pulled up outside their house at around six in the morning. Christine blinked into the strange gray haze outside the window. It had been over twenty-four hours since she had rushed to the hospital to meet Amanda and Audrey and Lola and Susan— over twenty-four hours since the immensity of her hope had lifted.

"How can one day feel like an entire year?" she asked Zach as he turned off the engine.

Zach didn't have an answer. He stepped outside the car, moved around to the passenger side, and helped Christine into the chilly air. This was the final day of February— February 28. When Christine stepped forward on wobbly legs, she whispered, "The baby's birthday is February 27. Isn't that a beautiful day to be born?"

She was talking nonsense now. Zach cast her a confused look as they entered the house.

"You should get some sleep," he told her. He helped her out of her winter coat and slung it over the chair nearest the foyer.

This wasn't the time to bother with front closet hangers. This wasn't the time for propriety or organization.

"Are you going to open the Bistro today?" Christine asked. This was maybe a question she would have asked any other day.

Zach grumbled and placed his hand across his forehead. "I don't know if I'm good to do anything today."

Christine wandered back into the kitchen. Zach called after her that she really should sleep, at least for a while. Christine somehow dreaded sleep. She feared that something would happen to Audrey and the baby while she slept. Besides, she also dreaded that horrible feeling— the moment you wake up in bliss and then have to remember the trauma you just went through. It had happened to her countless times, especially when she'd been a particularly heavy drinker.

For a while, her life had been on an awful constant loop: she'd go through a horrible breakup, or she'd get fired, or she'd get into a horrible fight with a friend, then she'd drink through the pain, pass out, and then awake to another day. The next day was even worse than the one before because she was hungover and even more self-hating.

No. It was better to stay awake until she had more information.

Zach disappeared for a while. Christine stood on uneasy legs in the kitchen. On the refrigerator, there was a little calendar Audrey had gotten them for Christmas, which told them the week-by-week growth of the baby. The current calendar read: Month 8.5. Too early. Not one of them had been emotionally ready. And the baby? He hadn't been physically ready.

Without thinking, Christine began to stir up cookie dough, just a traditional chocolate chip. Tears dripped down her cheeks as she continued. Just after she cracked the eggs, she poured herself a thick glass of merlot and sipped it. More morning light streamed in through the kitchen windows. She hadn't drank this early in years. It softened her racing, hard-edged thoughts. It made her limbs feel like jelly.

When she slotted the first tray of cookies into the preheated oven, she took another sip and wandered down the hallway. The house was eerily quiet. Normally, either Christine or Zach played music from one of the speaker systems. It was like they were in mourning.

Christine expected to find Zach in the bed they shared, but the room was dark and the bed was empty, the sheets all mussed from their quick get-away the previous early morning. She took another sip, turned back down the hallway, and then caught sight of Zach. She could see just the tip of his toes along the floor in the nursery.

She opened the door a bit more to allow a full view. Zach sat in the antique rocking chair, which they had bought at a garage sale the previous autumn. His head was bent forward, and he held a glass of whiskey in his right hand. He shifted the rocking chair back and forth with the soft tips of his toes. Christine hardly recognized his face. His sorrow made him look like a stranger.

"Hey."

Zach lifted his chin just the slightest bit. His youthful good looks had faded and were replaced with stress and anxiety.

"Hey," he returned.

"I put some cookies in the oven."

"Breakfast of champions," he replied.

Christine leaned heavily against the door jamb. "I just had to do something with my hands. We don't have to eat them."

Zach shook his head. A strange silence formed between them. Even an hour before, Christine might have stepped toward him and placed her hand on his shoulder and whispered that everything would be all right. Now, she felt she couldn't move any closer.

It was clear that Zach's mind was heavy with the baby he'd already lost.

This was a world Christine knew nothing about. This potential loss was strange and horrible but also fresh.

Probably, Zach's old wounds had been ripped open with the latest events.

She could practically see the trauma coming off him in waves.

"Can I get you anything?" she finally asked. Her voice cracked. How differently she'd imagined the day of the baby's birth! She had imagined herself and Audrey and Zach taking turns holding the baby and whispering excitedly and pinching themselves with disbelief at their own happiness.

Zach shook his head somberly. "Nope." He popped the "p" like an annoyed teenager. He wanted to be left alone.

Christine nodded before returning to the kitchen. She finished off her glass of wine and poured herself another. She removed the tray of cookies at precisely the right time. They were gooey, a soft golden color. She placed her teeth along the edge of one as the melted chocolate splayed out across her tongue.

She felt useless— utterly useless.

About an hour later, after two glasses of wine and a half-eaten cookie, Christine decided she couldn't stick around at home another moment longer. Zach's silence was deafening; the house shifted and quaked against the late February wind; and her sisters remained at the hospital, where she needed to be, too. As she didn't want to face Zach again, she penned a little note and stuck it on the fridge. After a pause, she removed the baby calendar from the fridge and stuck it in the trash under an empty package of flour.

Christine called a taxi. She stood in her driveway as soft snow billowed around her and stuck to her dark hair. She remembered her fear that once the baby was her responsibility, she would forget to dye her hair and end up like one of those frazzled mothers who didn't have time to take care of their appearance. Now, she was willing to trade her dark brunette hair for the wellness of that baby.

A "beautiful" Sheridan sister? What did it matter to her, what she looked like? All she wanted was her family's safety.

The taxi dropped her off. Christine walked her now-familiar zombie walk into the waiting room. There, she found that powerful and gorgeous Italian sailor, Tommy Gasbarro, all bent over, his face in his hands. Something about this man, defeated and so tired, broke Christine's heart even more. She placed the tupperware of chocolate chip cookies in the plastic chair beside him and said his name softly.

Tommy whipped a hand to the left and blinked up at her. After a pause, he dropped both hands and tried to smile. His lips failed him.

"Is Lola still in the room with Audrey?" Christine asked.

Tommy nodded. "She comes out from time to time to tell me to head back home. I can't bring myself to go, though." He paused and lifted the chocolate chip cookie container. "I hope you got some sleep. You weren't gone very long."

Christine shrugged. "It's basically impossible to sleep right now."

Christine turned to find Amanda and Susan coming out of the double-wide doors. Susan held a coffee and walked with her shoulders hunched, something Christine had never seen Susan Sheridan do in her entire life. Beside her, Amanda spoke in hushed, panicked tones. She held a croissant, one of the sad ones that the hospital cafeteria sold. To Christine, that was sacrilege: a stale, sad croissant, eaten on the saddest morning of the year.

"Christine. I can't believe you came back already," Susan said, just before she swallowed her up in a hug.

"Is there any news?" Christine asked.

Amanda shook her head. "Audrey should be awake in a little while. Aunt Lola really needs rest. I think she's delirious."

"None of us have gotten any sleep," Susan added. "Scott is threatening to kidnap me and take me back home."

With a jolt, Christine was reminded of something. "Where's Dad in all of this?"

"I had Aunt Kerry come pick him up that very first morning," Susan said. "There was no way it was healthy for him to be up here. He was tired and confused. He keeps calling me, though. He loves Audrey so much."

Amanda swiped her sleeve beneath her right eye. Even through her failed engagement and marriage, Christine hadn't seen her like this. She looked inconsolable.

"I was thinking about going to the office in a while," Amanda said suddenly. "We need to file that paperwork, and it's not like I can do anything here."

Both Christine and Susan said, "No," in unison.

"You shouldn't be alone right now. Not at the office. Not anywhere," Susan told her.

"Not until Audrey wakes up," Christine said.

Amanda's lower lip quivered as she struggled not to cry. She was like her mother; she wanted to be useful, but she felt utterly helpless.

At that moment, an enormous bouquet of flowers entered the waiting room. Behind them, Claire came into view— almost completely obstructed by the hugeness of the lilies. Behind her came her twins, Gail and Abby, and then Charlotte, Everett, and Rachel. Their eyes locked on Susan, Christine, and Amanda as they stepped toward them slowly, as though they were three injured animals and they didn't want to frighten them.

Suddenly, Claire placed the bouquet of flowers in Christine's hand. Charlotte said something like, "We are just so sorry," although Christine could hardly hear her over her own panic. Rachel, Gail, and Abby stood together and stared at the floor. They were only a few years younger than Audrey. Probably, they feared for what happened next in their own lives.

"Thank you," Susan said. She squeezed Charlotte's hand and turned toward Everett to nod. "It means a lot that you thought to stop by."

"Don't be silly, Susan," Claire said. "What can we do for you? You've already done so much for all of us in the Montgomery clan."

The next hour or so continued with a flurry of visitors. Camilla, Jennifer Conrad's good friend, who worked in the hospital, appeared to say hello and tell them that the nurses and doctors in the NICU were some of the best on the east coast. In time, Andrew's girlfriend, Beth, who also worked at the hospital, came down to ask if anyone needed anything to eat. Every greeting, every sorrowful hello, turned Christine's stomach.

She was so grateful that these people thought of them and wanted to be there for them. But there wasn't anything to say. Nothing could take the pain from their hearts.

Around eleven, Christine thought again of Zach. Susan and Amanda were in conversation with Claire and Charlotte, while Everett was off to the side playing a game with Rachel, Gail, and Abby. Tommy had eaten his weight in chocolate chip cookies and had his hand splayed over his stomach. Apparently, Scott was on his way.

Christine hoped that maybe, Zach would have the strength to come back to the hospital. She so needed him.

But when she called his cell phone, it went straight to voicemail.

She hoped he was sleeping. She hoped he was all right.

Chapter Seven

I t happened gradually, the eye-opening, as though she'd had her eyes closed for many years and had to relearn how to see. The light that poured in through her eyelids was soft and somber, and there was a sense that far off, perhaps beyond the nearest barrier, there was a wild world of rushing humans and panicked schedules. None of that existed here, in this ecosystem of quiet.

Audrey's eyes scanned down the ceiling above her, toward the television that hung in the corner and reflected back only the mirror image of the hospital room below. Slowly, Audrey's memory began to return to her. Slowly, the reality hit her across the chest.

She no longer had her baby inside of her. She'd given birth.

But where was her baby?

The white sheet that stretched out in front of her, over her still-bulbous but deflating stomach, was crisp and bright and alien. She placed her hands across the sheet and turned her head off toward her left. There, in the center chair, sat Amanda.

Amanda looked entirely un-Amanda-like just then. She had her mouth wide open; there was a bit of drool across her cheek; her feet were flung forward, as she'd apparently removed her boots; and her hair was tousled, but not in the "sexy beach wave" way. Audrey's heart panged with love for her cousin.

"Amanda?" she said softly. She didn't necessarily want to wake her, but she had to know what had happened. She couldn't live in limbo forever. "Amanda?" she said again, a little bit louder. "Amanda?"

Finally, Amanda jumped up as though Audrey had fished her out of a dream. She rubbed her eyes and then dropped her fists to find Audrey awake.

"Oh my God. You're up," Amanda breathed.

She reached out her hand and touched Audrey's tenderly. There was such sorrow in her eyes.

Audrey wanted to override the sorrow. Maybe, if she worked hard enough, or made enough jokes, whatever darkness had happened to her could be reversed. Maybe, if she was just one hundred percent herself, Audrey Sheridan, they would bring her baby daughter in and let her hold her. Maybe there was an explanation for all of this.

"You should have seen your face while you were asleep," Audrey teased. Her voice broke slightly, proof of how hard she tried. "Drool all over your chin. I should have taken a photo for blackmail."

How pathetic that she threatened blackmail from a hospital bed.

And Amanda's laugh sounded forced, as though she couldn't possibly find anything funny.

"What happened, anyway? Did my mom pay you to sit with me so she could go make out with Tommy or something?" Audrey continued.

Amanda rolled her eyes just the slightest bit. "She's obviously been right here almost the entire day. She just went to grab a bite to eat and put me in charge."

"Wow. Wait." Audrey's eyes jumped toward the window on the right side of the bed. The sun was on its way toward the horizon line. She had absolutely no idea what day it was. "What time is it?"

"It's getting close to six, I guess," Amanda said. Her lips stretched into a yawn.

"So, wait. When did I have my baby?" Audrey asked, trying to make sense of the time loss.

Amanda paused before she answered. "I guess it was around eighteen hours ago? Something like that."

"And I've been asleep since then?"

"They want to monitor you. There was some hemorrhaging after the placenta came out, but the nurse said that you're making a quick recovery." Amanda paused again, then asked, "Are you in any pain?"

Audrey considered this. There was a slight bit of pain, but nothing horrendous. In the back of her mind, she had flashing memories of the true pain, the pain of each contraction that felt like it was ripping her apart during the delivery. She blinked back tears as she forced herself to ask the question that was heaviest on her heart.

"Where is she?"

Amanda gripped Audrey's hand harder as though this could possibly mend her breaking heart. "The baby is very sick, Audrey."

Every muscle in Audrey's body clenched tight. For a long moment, she forgot to breathe.

Amanda kept going, as though she already knew what questions needed to be answered— as though she knew that Audrey couldn't possibly speak right then.

"It's called ARDS, apparently. It stands for acute respiratory distress syndrome. I guess he wasn't breathing when he was born, so they took him directly to the NICU for immediate monitoring and oxygen. I'm so, so sorry, Audrey. I'm so sorry."

For a long moment, Audrey couldn't register the words or make sense of how they fit into her reality. The amount of information was much more than she'd ever heard at one time.

Finally, she repeated back the disease, as though naming her enemy would give her power over it.

"Acute respiratory distress syndrome."

Amanda nodded. A single tear rolled down her cheek. "I went down to look at him through the glass, Audrey. He's so beautiful. Really, he is so beautiful."

Audrey bit hard on her lower lip and tasted blood. Her arms felt so heavy, as though they, too, thought they should be holding onto her baby.

"I don't know what to say," Audrey offered finally. "All my life, I've always known what to say. Right now, I can say for certain, that I'm speechless."

"You don't have to say anything," Amanda whispered.

"I don't understand. Was it something I did?" Audrey asked. Her face was etched with confusion as she struggled with the news. Her voice cracked again. "How did this happen, Amanda? Do you know? What did the doctor have to say?"

A moment later, Audrey tried to move, to get out of bed, but she let out a yelp of pain. "Goddammit," she cursed. Her head fell back against her pillow as she began to cry.

"Audrey, please," Amanda begged. "I don't want you to tire yourself out or make yourself sick. You've already been through so much."

Audrey closed her eyes, took a breath and opened them once again. For a second, she looked at her cousin as though she'd never seen her before in her life. But a second later, Amanda just smacked her thighs and said, "Audrey, we'll know more when the doctor updates us. We just want you to be okay. I just need you to be okay."

Suddenly, the door opened to reveal Grandpa Wes. He stood in the doorway for a moment as his eyes adjusted to the softness of the white room. Behind him, a nurse rushed through the hallway and then disappeared. Obviously, other people had bad days, too.

"Grandpa," Audrey said softly.

Through the previous eight months, she'd learned how to interact with her grandfather. Sometimes, his dementia made him a bit panicked; despite the ache of her soul, she didn't want to do anything that upset him.

"There they are," Grandpa Wes said as he slipped the door closed behind him and headed up toward the bed. "My two beautiful granddaughters. I should have known you'd be together."

Audrey stretched her hand out to grip his. It was a strong grip, one that had everything to do with a man and not with an aging dementia patient.

"Did Aunt Kerry just bring you back?" Amanda asked.

"She did," Grandpa Wes affirmed. "I told her I couldn't sit around her place talking to Trevor all day long. I needed to see my granddaughter and, of course, my new great-grandson."

For the first time, Audrey realized it. Both Grandpa Wes and Amanda had referred to the baby as a "he." She furrowed her brow and turned her eyes back toward Amanda.

"Did I have a boy?" she asked. For some reason, this felt like the strangest question of all.

Amanda swept a hand toward Audrey's hair to smooth it back toward the pillow. Before she could answer, Grandpa Wes did it for her.

"You did indeed, Audrey. A son." He clucked his tongue as his eyes shone with joy. "We wanted a boy that last time, you know? We had Susan and we had Christine, but then, we really, really wanted a boy to carry the Sheridan name and all. Anna and I prayed for it. I could see him so firmly in my mind,

51

you know? A little boy who loved train tracks and race cars and playing rough. But on that fateful day in August, your mother gave birth to Lola. And to be honest, when she was a little girl, she was something of a tomboy. In some ways, we did get a little boy that day. Anna and I used to joke that our prayers were half-answered."

In spite of everything, Audrey felt a laugh bubble up from her heart. She nestled her head deeper in her pillow.

"I have a little boy," she echoed.

"He is so perfect, Audrey," Amanda whispered. "Really. And such a little fighter. He's only been on this earth a day and already, he's gone through more than most of us have."

Audrey's lips parted. How could she possibly explain the depths of emotion she now felt? She'd been given the gift of a baby and had immediately learned a harsh lesson: that no matter what you did, sometimes, your baby had to fight to live.

"What did Christine say?" she finally asked. "About the baby?"

"She just wants you both to get well," Amanda replied.

Audrey's heart drummed heavily. In a strange way, she felt guilt for all this, for the pain that had been brought into the lives of the Sheridan family. She had gotten pregnant, and now, she'd forced this tremendous amount of love and fear into everyone's minds.

"Oh. I nearly forgot," Grandpa Wes said then. He reached into his back pocket and drew out a package of Fig Newtons, which had been Audrey's very favorite pregnancy snack early on.

"What the heck!"

Grandpa Wes splayed a perfect cookie onto her palm, then gave one to Amanda. "I thought of you when I saw them in Kerry's pantry. Don't tell her, but I stole them." He winked.

Amanda and Audrey giggled at that, although Audrey's laughter grew weaker with each passing moment. She ate the

Fig Newton slowly, appreciating every shift of flavor, every gooey bite. When she finished, she thanked her grandfather. And in return, he lifted her hand to his lips and pressed a kiss into her palm.

"You are a strong Sheridan girl," he told her, his eyes glassy. "You Sheridan women, you get through anything. I don't know how you do it. All I am is a big, old sap."

Chapter Eight

It was March 2, a full three nights after baby Sheridan was born. Audrey was discharged early, just after 9:30, and was wheeled out into the waiting area, where still, much of her family awaited her release. It was heart-wrenching to know that at just nineteen, she now faced one of the greatest hardships of her life.

Of course, Audrey wasn't the kind of girl to take pity on herself. None of the Sheridan girls were like that. It was in their blood, maybe, Christine thought.

Now, at 11 AM, Christine watched the poor girl, the young mother, as she gazed at her baby son through the glass at the NICU. Her face twitched strangely, as though she had to reckon with the idea that that little baby, hooked up to the oxygen machine, was the very one who'd grown in her belly all those months. When she turned back, her hand extended over her stomach, and her eyes shimmered with tears.

"I'm going to head home for a little while," she told Christine. "An hour or two. Shower and change and get my head on straight. Are you going to stay here?"

"For a little while," Christine told her.

Audrey nodded. She then turned back toward the double-wide doors and walked into the snowfall. Christine's heart ached for her. For a moment, she thought about jumping to her feet and running after her, telling her she couldn't go anywhere alone. But that very moment, Amanda pulled a car up to a halt at the curb. She jumped out, wrapped her arms around her cousin, and held her close. Snow billowed around them and made it difficult for Christine to see them completely. In a moment, they piled into the car, and then they rushed off, back to the house they shared with Wes Sheridan.

Christine was left alone with the baby she'd meant to care for.

There wasn't much you could see of him. It was essential that he was kept on machines at all times, and he was still too unstable for even Audrey to go to him, to hold him. Christine cupped her elbows and let herself really cry now.

The past few days had been nothing short of horror.

Since that first morning, Zach had been very quiet— the kind of quiet that Christine couldn't probe through. She'd sat at the edge of the bed the previous night and listened to his breathing as he'd slept. They hadn't opened the Bistro since the birth, and they hadn't even spoken about it, either, as though the decision was made by some other, unknown force. Through everything, Christine knew that Zach was swimming in his previous trauma with his daughter.

She prayed that once they got through this, he would find a way to go to therapy and deal with it head-on. Only then could he be the stand-in father this baby needed. Only then could Christine really imagine herself adopting more children with him and building a family.

But the idea that she had to create any kind of rule around this felt like a bruise to her soul. She loved Zach dearly. She just wanted everything to be okay.

Christine pressed her lips against her fingers and blew baby Sheridan a kiss. She then turned to walk down the hallway. She wanted a cup of coffee, maybe a snack, and then she could stand in front of that glass. Somehow, none of the Sheridans wanted baby Sheridan to sleep on without one of them present. They wanted him to know he was loved, that there was enough out there in the real world to stick around for.

Out by the coffee machine, Christine spotted Susan and Scott. Susan had her head on Scott's shoulder, and Scott read to her softly from a book of poetry he had in his outstretched hands. The view was so tender. It was a reminder that no matter what, Scott and Susan had the kind of love that would last forever.

Susan spotted Christine and whispered something to Scott. She then headed toward her, wrapped her in a hug, and said, "Gosh, what a day, huh?"

Christine nodded as the hug broke. "I guess we'll be saying that for a while."

"Audrey went home with Amanda," Susan said. "I'm glad she did, although I know she won't be gone for long."

"And how are you doing?" Christine asked as she pushed two quarters into the machine.

"Oh, you know. At my wit's end, really. I'm just so glad I hired that Sam guy to handle the stuff at the inn." Susan furrowed her brow, then added, "And I hope you know none of us blame you for not opening up the bakery and bistro. It's not a big deal. This is way more important."

Christine nodded. She wanted to tell Susan, at this moment, that she could hardly speak to Zach— that there was something much more wrong with him than she could fully describe. But instead, she just took her plastic cup, sipped the harsh, black liquid, and said, "I know. Thank you for saying that."

"I saw Zach go in there about an hour ago," Susan said. "I

tried to tell him that we don't need to open up. There's so much more to deal with. But he just kind of looked past me."

Oh. So, she already knew.

Christine pressed her lips together as silence fell between them.

Finally, she asked, "Do you think he's still there?"

Susan shrugged. "I don't know. I assume so. Why?" Her eyes demanded even more answers, like, *why don't you know where your boyfriend is? What's going on between the two of you? And why hasn't he been up to the hospital since the birth?*

But Susan Sheridan had tact. She could read the room. And she didn't ask.

"I guess I'll go check on him," Christine said. "Just to make sure he knows he shouldn't open up."

"That's probably a good idea," Susan said.

"But you'll sit with the baby? I don't think Audrey likes it when he's all alone in there."

"Of course," Susan replied. "Me and Scott will keep watch."

* * *

Christine drove the familiar route over to the Sunrise Cove Inn and Bistro. In his familiar parking spot, Zach had parked his car, and the sight made Christine's heart burst. It was both normal and completely not. It was like watching the sunrise and knowing it would be the last day on earth.

It was just past noon, which was normally a time when the doors whipped back and forth, and guests eased in and out for lunches with friends and family or business meetings. It felt strange and eerily quiet, entering those doors. But Christine soon found that she couldn't. They were still latched shut.

She turned left, sauntered down the sidewalk, and appeared at the front desk of the Sunrise Cove. Sometimes, if the light hit the foyer just right, she found it difficult not to imagine her mother, Anna, stationed at that very desk. But the man who peered back at her to greet her was Sam, the new, handsome twenty-something. Christine tried on a smile in return, but it felt false.

"Christine! Good to see you," Sam greeted her. He flung his fingers through his hair, then added, "I don't know how to say this, but I'm just really sorry about everything that's happened. Let me know if there's anything I can do."

Christine knew the appropriate thing to say was "thank you," but she couldn't muster the strength. Instead, her smile just fell, and silence flung itself between them. Awkward.

But a second or two later, Amanda popped out of the office. Christine was shocked to see her, as she'd thought she was back home with Audrey. Amanda's eyes scanned from Sam to Christine and back again.

"Aunt Christine. What are you doing here?"

"I just wanted to check on something at the bistro," Christine said. "Is Audrey okay?"

"She's fast asleep already," Amanda said. "Grandpa Wes, Charlotte, and Aunt Lola are all there, and I had to run a few errands for work. So here I am."

"I see," Christine said. Her eyes again returned to Sam, who, she knew, crushed hard on Amanda. The feelings were mutual, she thought, although so soon after Amanda's failed engagement, it seemed like the two of them planned to keep it slow.

Still, it was like there was a bubble of hope around them.

"Anyway. I'll say hi when I head out," Christine said as she headed down the hallway toward the bistro. "Don't work too hard, Amanda. You've been through a lot. We all have."

When she reached the bistro, she heard it: the speaker system in the kitchen blared loudly, as though there was a whole nightclub packed in there. Christine froze at the doorway. She glanced left toward the empty chairs and tables. A horrible thought came over her. Would they be able to take care of the bustling crowd again? Would she and Zach ever work side-by-side?

How had this all gone so terribly wrong?

Christine stepped toward the swinging door. After a deep breath, she pressed it open to find Zach.

He looked different than she'd ever seen him.

He leaned heavily against the walk-in fridge and banged his head strangely with the horrible, loud rock music that blared from the speakers. He had a glass of whiskey in one hand, and he wore stained chef's whites as though they were the only wardrobe he could find in his closet. When his eyes lifted toward her, they were red-tinged. They were proof of just how drunk he was. If Christine had to guess, he'd probably started drinking about five or six hours before.

"What the hell happened to you?" she breathed.

Zach gave her a horrible smile. For a moment, Christine was taken back to long-ago fights she'd had with her previous boyfriends in New York City. All of them had been borderline alcoholics; all of them had had anger problems. They'd always fought like cats and dogs.

Not her and Zach. They'd never been like that. Ever.

She had thought she'd broken the pattern.

"What do you mean, what the hell happened to me?" Zach demanded in a voice Christine hardly recognized. "I'm here, aren't I? Hell. We should open up the bistro, shouldn't we? I couldn't help but notice there's no freshly baked bread and no croissants, but we can make do. Can't we?"

Christine's heart dropped into her belly. "You're drunk."

"Of course I'm drunk," Zach spewed. "I've been drunk for days."

Christine's lower lip bounced. She had to keep it together.

She couldn't burst into tears in front of this borderline madman.

This was the man she loved. She had to remind herself of that.

They had to be there for each other.

"Zach, I know this has been really confusing and really hard for all of us," Christine whispered. "But we have to hold it together. The baby is sick, but he—"

"But what, Christine?" Zach demanded. He sauntered toward the counter, where he poured himself another two fingers of whiskey. "Then what? Now, I take care of a sick baby?"

Christine wanted to tell him that everything would be all right. It was no use, though. He'd already been through something that really hadn't turned out all right, and he was no fool. Pleasantries and "things you said" couldn't distract him from all that.

"Zach, babe, I know this is horrible for you," Christine tried. She stepped toward him as her heart pounded. "But Zach, we can do this. We can make this work. And once the baby gets out of the hospital—"

"And what if he doesn't get out of the hospital, Christine?" Zach spoke down toward his drink. "Then what?" He gasped for air as though his lungs struggled just like the baby's. He then lifted his glass, took a huge gulp of whiskey, and then turned to pummel the glass against the wall.

Glass shards sprung out every which way. Christine leaped back, totally panicked. She'd never seen Zach like this. As the glass settled down around them, Zach placed his head in his hands and moaned into them.

"I can't be a father again, Christine. I can't. It's too much. It's too much. I should have known. Not enough time has passed. I miss her. I miss her so much. I can't miss someone else. I can't."

It took a number of minutes, maybe even close to a half-hour, for Christine to get Zach into her car. She watched as he collapsed into the back seat. She was reminded of her mother, who'd seen her father in similar states throughout their marriage. *How had she dealt with it?*

Oh. Right. She'd had an affair.

But Christine loved Zach. She loved him with her whole heart. Zach needed her right then, just as she would certainly need him in the future. Resolute, she drove him back toward the house they shared, helped him to bed, and listened as his first early-afternoon snores rang out through the air.

When she reached the kitchen, she poured herself a glass of wine and nibbled on a cookie. She hadn't eaten anything in terms of "meals" in the last seventy-two hours, it seemed like.

She had no idea how any of them would make it through this. But she knew they just simply had to.

Chapter Nine

Audrey awoke. There was always this first, beautiful, hazy part of the morning when she was allowed to feel and think and act just like a nineteen-year-old college student, a woman with her grip on the world. But all that crashed down around her the moment she felt it: the subtle pain, the fear that her baby, over in the NICU, wouldn't make it through the night.

Slowly, she removed herself from bed, then turned to find Amanda alongside her. Audrey had forgotten that, too: that she'd crawled into bed the previous night with Amanda, longing to be close to anyone. She had asked Amanda to tell her a story while she fell asleep, and she'd done it. Amanda had told Audrey the extended story of how she'd first met her ex-fiancé, Chris, and fallen in love. Just before she had fallen asleep, Audrey had whispered, "Isn't it painful to talk about this? You can choose another story." But Amanda had said, "Actually, I'm in the process of trying to appreciate the story around Chris while knowing that we weren't right for each other. Every person comes into our life for a reason. Don't you think?"

"I hope so," Audrey had breathed as she'd drifted off. "I really do."

Now, on this fresh morning, Amanda reached for her phone and read the time. "Babe, it's only five. We should rest a little bit more, don't you think?"

"What? No." Audrey slowly slipped out of bed and made her way out of the first-floor bedroom and headed up to her room, where she dressed in a pair of leggings and a big Penn State sweatshirt. After a pause, she slid some eyeliner around her eyes and placed some blush over the apples of her cheeks. Even though she wasn't trying to impress anyone, she wanted to look a little better than how she felt.

There was that wishful thinking again.

Downstairs, Amanda rubbed her eyes and shrugged herself into a coat. When she glanced up, she said, "You did your makeup."

Audrey shrugged. "It's not the first time I've dressed up for a guy."

Audrey told Amanda she didn't have to go to the hospital with her so early, but Amanda wouldn't hear of letting her go alone. Everyone in the Sheridan family regarded Audrey like a little lost dog or a toy that was on the verge of breaking. She hated it. She was nearly twenty years old, and she'd just given birth, for Pete's sake. She wanted more power over her life again.

Once at the NICU, Audrey rushed toward the glass to spot her little boy. She pressed her fingers on the glass and felt her heart fall through her ribcage and through the space between her and her son. "I love you. I love you so completely," she whispered.

A few minutes later, Amanda joined her, bleary-eyed. She

passed her a cup of bad coffee and a packaged muffin, cinna-mon-flavored.

"I think he's getting better," Audrey whispered as she took the coffee. "I can feel it."

Amanda's eyes didn't know what to do with that informa-tion. She cast them down toward the coffee. After a small moment of silence, she said, "That's good," then added, "I think I might be getting used to this coffee. Is that crazy?"

At just past nine, Christine and Lola joined them. Audrey fell into the hug with her mother and breathed the words into her ear, as well. "I think he'll be okay. I can just feel it."

But of course, nobody could believe her. She wasn't a doctor.

At ten, Christine, Lola, and Audrey met with the baby's doctor. With stale, flat words, he explained that baby Sheridan had to remain on oxygen for a number of days more. This sent Audrey's heart into a dark place.

"But when can we take him home?" Audrey demanded. She hated how panicked she sounded.

The doctor's words remained somber. "I don't know yet. We're monitoring him at every stage. Sometimes, these things take time. But in the meantime, this will allow you to heal and regain your strength. Once he comes home, you'll be busy."

When they left the office, Audrey felt listless and strange. Christine's face reflected back the same emotions. Her mother looked at both of them with shock etched over her forehead.

Audrey sat on the bench outside of the NICU and blinked at the glass for a long time. Minutes passed. Occasion-ally, she had to get up and pump the milk from her breasts, which had grown into a near-constant annoyance. She hated it, especially when she threw the milk down the drain— what a waste.

Just past one, Lola admitted she had to run off to meet Tommy for something. She kissed Audrey's forehead and said she would see her in a few hours. "I'll text you. Have your phone on you," she insisted.

This left only Christine and Audrey, the two "mothers" of the ailing baby. Christine looked just as depleted as she had when Audrey had first met her the previous summer. Martha's Vineyard had initially filled her with light. That light now seemed to be gone.

"I think we should go get some food," Christine finally said. Her voice was low, strange.

Audrey coughed once and then felt a wave of horror and fear. Christine grabbed her arm and asked, "What's wrong? Are you okay?"

Audrey's hand went to her crotch, and then she started laughing. "I think my vagina just fell out after that cough."

Christine laughed alongside her niece as their moods lightened a little.

"Come on. We should eat something. I haven't really fed myself in days, either."

When they walked into the light of the early afternoon in early March, Audrey immediately noticed a strange shift in temperature. The previous day had been frigid and winter-like, but this, on the other hand, had a touch of spring to it. Audrey wasn't sure how to feel. On the one hand, she resented the fact that the seasons could go on without her son. On the other, she longed for spring, for summer, for the freedom the sun brought along with it.

Christine led her toward a little restaurant situated along the waterline. Before they entered, Audrey glanced left toward the docks that spread out near the hospital. She remembered her mother's story of how she'd first encountered Tommy out on those docks— how she'd just walked up to him and demanded his attention. The brashness of Lola Sheridan! She wished she could bottle it and take it as a pill. Especially right then.

Christine and Audrey sat near the back, with a perfect view of the springtime waters. Christine ordered a glass of Italian wine while Audrey opted for apple juice, along with gourmet sandwiches, olives, fresh fruit, and dessert. Audrey ate slowly. With each delicate bite, something in her told her she didn't deserve such beautiful foods. Everything was delicious, though, and she was grateful that she could leave reality behind for a moment.

With every moment that passed, Audrey felt sure there was something really wrong with Christine. But before she could ask, Christine turned a question on her instead.

"Why haven't you named him yet?"

Audrey's lips opened with surprise.

But Christine continued. "If it's because you're afraid it will jinx it, I don't think you should be afraid. That baby has been on this planet since February 27, and he deserves a name to call his own. Maybe it will give him something to cling to. I don't know."

Tears sprung to Audrey's eyes. She knew how right her aunt was.

"I just. I hadn't even. I—" "She stuttered for a moment, then continued. "I hadn't even considered any names for boys— only for girls."

Christine chuckled sadly. "You were so sure."

"I really was."

"Why were you so sure? Because Susan and your mom said you were carrying high? That's just an old myth."

Audrey shook her head. "Youthful ignorance, maybe. I thought all of life would be exactly as you planned it. But in fact, the surprise pregnancy should have been proof enough that life doesn't work like that."

Audrey scrunched up her nose and again sipped her juice. "But a baby boy. I really just never thought I could. I'd always heard stories about my grandmother, Anna Sheridan. And then, I grew up with my mother. And I just felt that I wanted to extend that line."

"The three of you do look exactly alike," Christine affirmed. "It's uncanny."

"But maybe he'll have a different look," Audrey breathed. With a jolt, she sat up straighter in her chair and said, "Actually, maybe he'll look like Grandpa Wes!"

The idea surprised her and then excitement washed over her. Christine actually laughed, although she looked as though she didn't fully want to.

"That's something you want, isn't it?" Christine asked.

"So, so much," Audrey said. "Grandpa Wes has been one of my greatest friends this past year. While the frat parties rage on, me and Grandpa Wes eat M&Ms in peace and share old stories."

Audrey was also surprised by this sentiment. Had she made a joke? She hadn't made one of those in days.

Maybe it was the springtime sun.

Maybe it was hope.

"I'll think of a name," Audrey said softly. "Something that will suit him perfectly."

She rested her chin against her chest and pondered it for a long time. Occasionally, Christine spit out various names.

"What about Oscar?"

"Yuck," Audrey said.

"Timothy?"

"Are you kidding me?"

"Adrian."

"What! No."

The conversation lingered on for quite some time until suddenly, out of nowhere, Audrey said, "Maxwell," and their eyes locked. There was something so powerful about it.

Maxwell Wesley Sheridan. They said his name over and over again. Maxwell Wesley Sheridan.

"I love it. We can call him Max for short." Audrey beamed. "It's perfect."

Just as Christine lifted her wallet to pay for the wine and food, Susan Sheridan burst in through the far door and growled at them. "Where have you been?"

Audrey looked at her aunt with surprise.

"Relax, Susie," Christine said with a bright smile.

Susan paused at their table and turned her eyes from Christine to Audrey and back again. "What's gotten into you two?"

"Well, for one, we finally ate a good meal," Christine replied. "Which solved quite a few of our issues."

"And for two, we named the baby!" Audrey cried.

All the tension fell from Susan's face. She dropped her hands to either side of her waist and blinked at them with huge eyes.

"Are you going to tell me?"

Christine scrunched her lips together while Audrey said, "I don't know. Are you going to keep yelling at us?"

Susan rolled her eyes. "I just wanted to let you know that we're planning a big family dinner at the house. You should both be there. We need you."

Audrey and Christine locked eyes again.

"What do you think, Momma?" Christine asked.

Audrey shrugged. "I think we have to make a pit stop at the hospital. Max can't go another hour without his legal name. Don't you think?"

Audrey watched her aunt's frown turn into a huge smile. "I love it! It's absolutely wonderful. Is Max short for Maxwell?"

Audrey nodded with a smile. "Middle name, Wesley."

It was a remarkable thing to fill out that birth certificate. Audrey shivered when it was finalized. She then marched toward the glass at the NICU and spoke Max's name to him, under her breath, as sweetly as she could.

"Welcome to the world, Max Wesley Sheridan. There is so much in store for you once you get out of there. And we love you so much."

Chapter Ten

The house was full yet again. Christine stepped into the bustling atmosphere as if she was having an out-of-body experience. Her father, Wes, told a vibrant story to her Uncle Trevor in the corner and swung his arms around; Aunt Kerry busied herself in the kitchen, hovering over a large pot of lemon chicken soup with tortellini; Lola was cozied up alongside Tommy, her eyes hazy. The trauma of this birth had done a number on all of them, but there was a real power transmitted here, in the heart of their home. Anything could happen.

Lola jumped up and hugged Audrey close. The tender kiss she placed on Audrey's forehead made Christine turn away. She hated to admit her occasional jealousy over Lola and Audrey's relationship, especially given how close she now felt to Audrey.

"We named him, Mom!" Audrey said as she stepped back.

"What's that?" Grandpa Wes called from the corner. "Does my grandson finally have a name?"

Silence fell over the room. Expectation etched itself across each and every Sheridan and Montgomery face.

"I named him Max. Maxwell Wesley Sheridan," Audrey finally said as she snapped her hands together with pride. Her eyes found her grandfather, who had tears in his eyes.

"You gave him my name," Wes murmured.

"It's perfect for him, Grandpa," Audrey said, giving him a tender smile.

Joy flung through the room. Lola hugged Audrey yet again, and Susan came to hug Christine, who closed her eyes and felt herself shake with strange relief. Somehow, now that the baby had a name, the universe had shifted in their favor. They weren't out of the woods yet, though.

"It's a great name," Susan said as she fell back. She continued to grip Christine's shoulders as she peered into her eyes. "How are you feeling?"

Probably, the massive under-eye shadows and devastation from the baby and the situation with Zach didn't make Christine a beauty contest candidate. Susan Sheridan could see directly through her. She'd always been able to.

"It's not a big deal," she insisted. "Just some trouble sleeping."

"I hope you're eating enough," Susan said.

"Audrey and I had a pretty big meal for lunch," Christine said.

"And you'll eat more later on," Susan insisted. "That lemon chicken soup that Aunt Kerry made is delicious, maybe even better than her chowder." She squeezed at Christine's upper arms as though her hands alone could sense any unhealthy weight loss. "Is Zach on his way over?"

The words were glass shards, and they flung through Christine's heart and tore it into slices. Christine swallowed the lump in her throat and heard herself answer, "He might be busy tonight. He said he might not make it. But I guess I'll call him

71

again, just to make sure. I don't know a single man who can resist Aunt Kerry's cooking."

"Call him," Susan said softly. "I'm sure he doesn't want to be alone in this, either."

Ah. How wrong you are, Susan Sheridan! Christine so longed to say this. But she cut her teeth into her bottom lip and sauntered out toward the mudroom, where she made yet another call to Zach Walters. The phone rang and rang. She pressed her ear with her finger a bit too hard as she waited in order to drown out the vibrant laughter from the other room. Where the heck was he? Why couldn't he answer the phone?

Just as she hung up, cousin Andy, Beth, and her son, Will, snuck through the door. Beth, ever the kind soul, said a bright, "Hello!" as she stepped toward Christine and hugged her tight. Christine hadn't seen her since the day after the delivery when Beth had stopped by the waiting room.

"So glad you guys could make it!" Christine said as the hug broke. She felt how empty her words were. Her eyes turned toward little Will, who looked up at her with that same serious, inquisitive nature. It was like he could see directly through her all the time. It was a little eerie.

"I heard about your baby," Will said finally.

Beth's face looked pained, but Christine was grateful that he'd spoken the truth.

"Yes. He's very sick," Christine finally returned.

"Do you think he will get better?" Will asked.

Christine's heart drummed in her throat. "I hope so. But I don't really know."

Beth squatted down beside Will and brushed his hair over his ear gently. "We've kept baby Sheridan in our thoughts, haven't we?"

Will nodded as Christine said, "Audrey named him. She named him Max."

"Max!" Will said a bit too loudly. "That is a superhero's name."

Beth and Christine made eye contact. A funny smile spread between Christine's cheeks. Somehow, he was right. It was a superhero's name. A very particular, new kind of superhero. The kind that had to take on the world before he knew anything in it.

Another table was brought into the living area, just a few feet from the kitchen table. Christine busied herself, setting up the plates and wine glasses and slicing the bread. She detested that this particular bread was store-bought since she hadn't had time to bake anything recently, but nobody else seemed to notice. When they sat, and everyone took a slice on their plate except for her, Audrey teased her and said, "Is this bread not good enough for our world-famous baker, Christine?"

Christine flashed her an ominous smile. "Don't get me in trouble," she teased as she lightly kicked Audrey beneath the table.

"Oh dear me," Aunt Kerry said. She lifted the bread to eye-level to analyze the seeds and grains within. "Is this bread really not so good? I bought the one with nineteen different kinds of grains!"

"We're just so spoiled with your bread, usually," Uncle Trevor said to Christine.

"Spoiled with it? I've gained like five pounds since I got back to the Vineyard in December," Andy added.

"Only five? I guess we're not trying hard enough," Susan said as she smeared some butter across her piece of bread. "And Aunt Kerry, don't you worry about the bread. I think it's delicious."

"Well, it isn't my specialty," Aunt Kerry said.

"You've only got the best lemon chicken soup and clam chowder on the island, Mom," Kelli interjected. "I think that, in and of itself, is a skill to be proud of."

It was funny, Christine thought, to fall into these easy conversations. They were words that might have been said at any given time, in any given season, but they were oddly soothing now, especially with baby Max in the hospital. Audrey ate heartily and said she planned to continue to be pregnant with a "food baby" as long as she could manage it. At this, Susan rolled her eyes and said, "You'll be right back to normal in a snap, my dear. Nothing like that nineteen-year-old metabolism."

"Almost twenty years old, I'll have you know," Audrey said.

"Oh! We should plan a party," Amanda said brightly. "Twenty is huge."

"I remember when I turned twenty," Lola said with a sigh. "Audrey was just a little bouncing ball of baby energy. I was barely conscious."

Audrey's lips curved downward just the slightest bit. Several people at the kitchen table and the living room table turned their eyes toward the soup. Lola reached over and squeezed her daughter's hand, then said, "And I'm sure baby Max will be here for your big day, too."

Audrey's eyes welled with tears, but she blinked them back and placed her spoon in the soup again. At the other table, Steven began to talk about something that had happened at his auto shop earlier in the week, which was yet another boring conversation that everyone could cling to. Normality was best. Normality was what they needed most.

After Christine spooned herself one-half of her bowl of lemon chicken soup, she again excused herself to the backroom to call Zach. The phone rang and rang and rang. Outside, night had crept up and cast the driveway in a strange, gray light. The snow had melted, and the grass beneath was lifeless and brown. With a heavy heart, Christine collected her coat and walked to her car. Once at the wheel, she knew what she had to do.

When she pulled up in front of the house she'd shared with Zach all these months, she sensed an emptiness to it. Zach's car wasn't in the driveway; the garage seemed hollow. She forced herself up the driveway and down the walkway and then into the front door. Although she knew there would be no answer, she still said, "I'm home!" like she was some character in a sitcom.

But this was no sitcom. This was the sad result of a life she'd wanted so badly. It was like they'd gotten the math wrong.

Christine entered the kitchen, where she discovered a half-drunk bottle of whiskey next to a used glass. Beside it, there was a note. It was folded up. Christine half-hated him for folding it. In some respects, she could have gone the rest of her life without unfolding it. Unfolding it to know what he'd actually written felt like looking at the sun.

Christine poured herself the slightest glass of whiskey. It was almost like he'd left the bottle right there just for her.

Then, she unfolded.

It read: *I'm sorry. I need to think.*

And that's all.

Christine crumpled the note with her fist and stared at the wall for a long time. She couldn't make sense of this. Just a week ago, they'd curled up in bed and whispered sweet nothings and spun in excitement for this baby, this baby that they planned to raise together. Now, he'd left without the decency to tell her exactly where he planned to go.

It felt as though someone had torn through her ribcage, squeezed her heart from its place, and slowly, terribly, dragged it out into the air.

In some ways, she wished someone would actually do that, just so the pain actually meant something.

Christine fell to the floor after that. She remembered her past belief that Sheridan women were strong, stronger than any other women she knew. It was like her body wanted to disprove that. She blinked into nothingness for maybe ten minutes, maybe an hour. Sometime later, she heard footsteps in the foyer. And in a moment, Susan and Lola stood in front of her, both dressed in thick winter coats, with large hats on their heads. They'd come looking for her. They'd found her. But she was nothing much to look at.

Lola dropped to a squat in front of her, gripped her hands, and said, "Christine? Chris? Are you okay? Can you hear me?"

Christine nodded somberly. After a pause, she said, "I was just about to come back to the house."

Above Lola, Susan said, "We were just a little bit worried about you."

"You shouldn't have worried about me. I just stepped out for a minute," Christine lied.

Lola turned her head up to make eye contact with Susan. It seemed like they had some kind of conversation through the air, one that Christine was too messed up to understand.

"Let's get you back home, huh?" Lola finally said. "Oh. And your cat! Felix! Felix?"

The orange tabby hustled in from wherever he'd been hiding. He shivered against Christine's shins and meowed brightly, greeting the newcomers.

"He always shows off," Christine said.

"Audrey will be so happy to have the kitty back," Lola said. "We'll get a little more morale in the house."

Christine was listless as she packed a bag for herself, arranged the kitty litter in the back of Lola's car, and scrambled into the backseat like a child. Susan and Lola discussed a new restoration project happening outside of Edgartown as they drove. One of Jennifer Conrad's friends, Olivia Hesson— a teacher at the Edgartown High School, had been given a historic building by her great-aunt and had decided to build it up into a boutique hotel.

"I saw her at the store the other day," Lola affirmed. "She said she feels like she's lost her mind."

"Welcome to the hospitality business," Susan said. "Right, Christine?"

But Christine didn't have the strength to answer. She wrapped her arms around her body and shivered with apprehension. *Where had Zach gone? Had he left the island? Would he ever return?*

And if he ever came back, could she really forgive him for what he'd now done? He had abandoned her when times were rough, just like so many of her other stupid, alcoholic chef boyfriends. Why had she thought he was any different? Was she really that gullible?

Chapter Eleven

I t had been two days since the dinner party at the Sheridan house. Audrey stood with a mug of steaming coffee and again watched the waters beyond the dock. It seemed incredible that her baby had been born nearly a week before, as, throughout that week, the weather had shifted considerably. New types of birds had made their appearance (much to the delight of Grandpa Wes), and the general "feeling" of everyone tinged toward springtime optimism. Of course, any kind of springtime optimism Audrey showed to others was something of an act.

Her son remained in the NICU, and there was no telling when he would come home with her. Nothing else mattered.

Well, almost nothing. On the night of the party, Aunt Susan and her mother had brought home a severely depressed, half-drunken Christine, who finally reported, after a lot of coaxing, that Zach had left her. This definitely put a hiccup in their plan moving forward. One: Audrey was heartbroken over Christine's depression. The woman had been through enough over the years; she certainly didn't need this. Two: Audrey had planned to have Christine and Zach team up to raise her baby. Obviously, Zach couldn't handle it, and Christine's eyes were so hollow with pain that she wasn't sure she could manage it, either.

Of course, all these thoughts were getting ahead of everything else. The added stress was taking its toll on everyone. Max had to heal first. He had to grow stronger.

Amanda stepped out of her bedroom and stretched her arms high above her head. Already, she'd dressed in her work outfit for the day, styled her hair, and done her makeup. It was just past six in the morning, but she'd grown accustomed to Audrey's set-upon routine. She wanted to be at the hospital early. She didn't want to miss a thing.

On the drive to the NICU, they spoke softly about Aunt Christine, as though she could hear them.

"I hope she's comfortable in that old bed," Amanda whispered. "It's got that awful dip in the middle. And she didn't come down for dinner last night. Not that you ate hardly anything, either." She gave Audrey a scolding glance.

Audrey shivered, despite the thickness of her coat. "I tried to talk to her a bit after dinner, but she just mentioned something about it not being Zach's fault."

"Bull. It's obviously Zach's fault," Amanda snapped back. She gripped the steering wheel hard so that her knuckles turned bright white. "Who else is to blame? Whose fault could it be?"

"I mean, it's so complicated, right? Because he lost his toddler." Audrey's throat tightened at the thought. She couldn't bear the thought of actually losing her baby. Right now, she was in limbo. They knew nothing for sure. But Zach's toddler had left the world for good.

"I know, but this is an entirely new situation, and he has to be here for you and Christine," Amanda tried to reason with her. "He promised he would be."

Audrey sighed. "I know. He did. But I don't think every-thing is as black and white as you do. I think this entire situa-tion has ripped open his old wound."

Amanda's nostrils flared. This was typical Type-A behav-ior, Audrey knew. Amanda expected everyone to uphold the rules above all things. She expected people to keep their word. This was admirable, but it wasn't always possible. People were messy. Amanda had learned this first-hand when her fiancé had left her at the altar, quit his job, and ran off on a round-the-world adventure. Audrey knew better than to bring up Chris right then, though. There was already enough pain to go around.

Amanda and Audrey sat outside the NICU for a good hour without speaking. Amanda went over some of her notes for both her online law school classes and her appointments at the law firm she'd started with her mother. Audrey had her hands folded over her lap, and her eyes focused on the glass. Again, her heart banged against the very front of her ribcage, as though it could jump out and crawl over to her son.

Sam from the Sunrise Cove, of all people, arrived a little after seven-thirty. He met them just outside the NICU with two coffees and two donuts. He hugged Amanda close, a bit too close, in fact, then said, "Audrey. It's so good to see you again."

Audrey took the bag of donuts and smiled at him, this handsome man her cousin crushed on. "Thank you for the donuts. Are they Frosted Delights?"

"The best on the island," Sam affirmed. "And when I said they were for the Sheridan girls, Jennifer gave them to me for free. I'm not from the Vineyard, but I already get to use the Sheridan family name as currency around here. It's an awesome perk."

"Yes. We're definitely well known," Audrey replied with a slight smile.

Audrey left Amanda and Sam to speak alone and returned

to the glass outside the NICU. She nibbled on the edge of a donut, even as her stomach gurgled with hunger. Maybe a different version of herself would have stuffed the whole thing into her mouth.

Amanda returned a bit later. Her cheeks brightened to a shade of pink as she collected her donut.

"Sam came to the hospital to see you!" Audrey stated incredulously. She said it because she knew Amanda really didn't want her to point it out.

Amanda shrugged. "I haven't seen him in a few days. I've just been so busy with the family and school and the firm."

"I get it." Audrey paused for a moment. "And it's sweet he thought of you."

"He works for my mom. He has to think of me," Amanda said.

Audrey wanted to ask just when Amanda would stop pretending she wasn't into Sam. But before she could, Amanda stood, placed the rest of her donut into the little brown bag it had come in, and said she had to get over to the law office. "You'll be okay here by yourself for a while? I can come back in a few hours."

"It's not a problem," Audrey replied. In fact, she'd grown pretty tired of everyone doting on her all the time. She wanted space to think her own thoughts. She wanted time to dream up Max's future. Somehow, building a world of positivity around this little baby made her feel she had more power over the situation. It was prayer, maybe, or some kind of fate that was already written. She would accept whatever worked.

When Amanda left, Audrey slipped her donut into the brown bag, crossed her arms over her chest, and stretched her legs out in front of her. She sat like a teenager in a high school classroom who waited for the bell to ring. It hadn't been so long ago that she had been exactly that, all the way back home in Boston. When had she stopped really feeling that Boston was her home? She'd grown up there. Everything in her life had been there. Now, she felt her entire life was firmly rooted in the Vineyard. How strange.

Around eleven-thirty, Amanda texted to say she'd gotten held up in a meeting, but she would be back at the hospital in about an hour. Audrey had hardly noticed the passing of time. She had eaten the rest of her donut hours ago, but her stomach still grumbled ominously, and she stepped toward the vending machine to inspect the selection. She wrapped herself tightly in her coat as she analyzed the various cookies and candies and pretzels. It was a funny thing; in the reflection of the vending machine glass, she just looked like a normal nineteen-year-old girl. Beneath the coat, she didn't look pregnant at all.

She had longed to look "not pregnant" for months. Now, she had her wish.

Audrey leafed through her purse for change, which was mostly concealed in crumbs at the bottom. As she searched, a guy in his early twenties, maybe, stepped toward the vending machine and clucked his tongue. Audrey's eyes flipped up toward his face, which had this classic Roman nose, these beautiful, dark eyes, and a rugged, five-o-clock shadow, which made him look even more handsome.

"What should my lunch be?" he said to nobody in particular. "Pretzels or peanuts or just straight for the sweet stuff?"

Audrey shrugged, lifted three quarters, and plunked them in, one after another. With a funny smile, she pressed F17 and watched as a bag of Reese's Pieces began to crank out from its prison.

"Straight to the sweets for you, then?" the guy asked.

"I don't like to mess around."

"I appreciate that in a person. You should always get what you want."

"I agree."

But that moment, just as the package of candies was meant

to drop below, the little, jagged edge of the machine caught it and held onto it as if its life depended on it. Audrey's smile fell immediately.

"No!"

"What a scam," the guy said.

"Seriously. First, medical bills, and now, this?" Audrey huffed at the glass.

The guy laughed appreciatively. "Come on. You aren't going to let this take advantage of you, are you?"

Audrey furrowed her brow. "As a rule, I never let anyone take advantage of me."

"That's what I thought," the guy said, although he was a perfect stranger.

"Let's shake it," Audrey suggested. "We either break it, or we free my candy. I'm good either way."

They stepped on either side of the machine, gripped the edges, and then counted to three. The first few tips forward were fine, but the fourth made Audrey wheeze with pain. She wasn't completely healed from the delivery yet. It had been silly to think she was back to her normal self.

"You okay?" the guy asked as he cranked the machine forward on his own.

This last tip did the trick. The bright orange package dropped to the belly of the beast. Audrey nodded and grinned. "I just wanted to see if you could do it by yourself."

"Ah. A test. I love tests," he teased, giving her a lopsided grin.

Audrey had to sit. She grabbed her candy and retreated toward the nearest chair, where she watched the guy pick out a package of Oreos. When he turned back, his eyes connected with hers, and he asked, "Do you mind if I sit with you?"

"Not at all," Audrey said.

Without speaking, they both tore open their packages.

Audrey let her first Reese's Pieces droplet melt against her tongue. The peanut butter was almost too sweet.

"Man, what a wild night," the guy finally said.

"Yeah?" Obviously, there was a reason he sat outside the NICU. There weren't good reasons to sit outside of the NICU.

"Yeah. My mom had a baby last night. She's forty-three, so it was already kind of a scary thing. And then the baby had some trouble breathing, and they rushed her here, and, well. Now, my mom is resting, and I didn't want my baby sister to be alone, you know?"

He bit on the edge of his Oreo. For the first time, Audrey recognized the red tinge in his eyes. He was exhausted.

"That sounds really hard," Audrey whispered.

"Yeah. It's so weird," he admitted. He then glanced toward her, furrowed his brow, and asked, "You must have a brother or sister in there, too?"

Audrey nodded. Why did she nod? Why did she agree? It just seemed easier, somehow, to put the pain on some other, fictional person. "I don't want him to be alone, either."

"It's weird since they don't really know what being alone even means," the guy said. "They've just been attached to their mother the entire time. And now, they're alone in that room."

"Yup. They're in that room," Audrey repeated.

Silence fell over the two of them then. Audrey's heart thudded with sadness and fear. After a while, the guy admitted he had to go check on his mother. Audrey said her cousin was about to return, anyway. They nodded their goodbyes, grateful to have someone to share this pain with. And then, in a moment, the stranger was gone.

Chapter Twelve

Max Sheridan was one week old. It was as though the weather had planned ahead for such an achievement, as it brought bright blue, clear skies, sharp sunlight, and the first few buds on a tree that had gotten ahead of itself, just outside the Sunrise Cove. Christine stood in the splendor of the sun with her chin lifted. She had baked croissants, and she held the bag with one hand and a mug of coffee in her other. She hadn't heard from Zach in days, and the thought of it made her stomach heave with sadness. But the springtime weather— that was at least something to cling to.

Christine stepped into the foyer to say hello to Susan and Sam, who was in the midst of a discussion about a particularly unruly guest at the Sunrise Cove.

"They played techno music until one in the morning," Sam explained as he rolled his eyes. "I told them over and over again that this is a family inn. Not a party place. And I mean, who comes to Martha's Vineyard in March to party like that?"

"You should have been here when Ursula had her wedding on the island," Christine told him with a smirk. "So many people were arrested for being rowdy. Susan, you should have had your law office up and running back then. You'd have gotten a lot of clients."

"I had thought about that," Susan said with a laugh. "But we were all so exhausted from that crazy wedding. I don't think I could have managed to do anything but sleep."

There was also the fact that Susan had only just recovered from cancer around then. Exhaustion had made it difficult for her to do much of anything. More and more, as spring brightened around them and time passed, Susan Sheridan looked like herself— that force of nature, that beautiful queen.

"Are you headed to the hospital?" Susan asked.

"Yes. Audrey, Lola, and I are meeting with the doctor."

"Let me know when you know more," Susan said. "I'll be at the law office later. Don't hesitate to call."

"We won't."

Christine walked over to the hospital, where she found Lola and Audrey stationed outside of the doctor's office. Audrey was all wrapped up in a coat, shivering, with her eyes toward the door. Lola seemed anxious, telling a story that neither of them seemed to care about, about a story she had to write for the *Boston Tribune*. Lola had told Christine that it was the worst thing in the world to take stories just then but that she just needed to put her mind elsewhere, beyond the baby and her worries about Audrey. "I have to write. It's the only thing I have," she'd said.

Christine tried to give her croissants to the girls, but both admitted they were too nervous to eat. Christine was, too. She had only baked them due to the quivering anxiety of her own heart. Minutes later, the doctor called them in, and she held the package of croissants on her lap, feeling foolish.

"Good morning," the doctor said. "I trust this has been a very difficult few days for all of you. But I want you to know that everything has gone exactly to plan."

Audrey inhaled sharply. "What do you mean?"

"The baby's oxygen levels are improving," the doctor continued. "If all continues like this, we should be able to release him in about a week."

Audrey's shoulders fell forward. A strange cry fell from her lips. Lola spread her hand across her shoulder and whispered, "It's going to be okay. He's going to be okay."

"And what about long-term effects?" Christine asked. She'd read a little bit about this on the internet, although the idea terrified her.

"Often, the baby can make a full recovery, so much so that there aren't any signs of this later in life," the doctor continued. "But again, these are still early days. We will continue to monitor him closely."

Even still, there was an air of relief when the three Sheridan women stepped out of the doctor's office. Audrey's knees clacked together, and she admitted that she might collapse on the ground if she didn't get something to eat. Christine passed over a croissant, which Audrey shoved into her mouth as she burst into tears.

"I really need to sleep," she said finally as she swallowed the last morsel. "I couldn't sleep at all last night because I was so worried about this meeting."

"Why don't you go home?" Lola suggested, rubbing the small of Audrey's back. "Tommy can drive you over. Christine, you want to head back, too?"

They stepped into the parking lot to find Tommy idling in his truck. He stepped out and hugged each of them, then helped Audrey get comfortable in the back seat. It was a tight fit, but Audrey was a tiny thing, and she managed it.

"You're dressed in your sailing garb, aren't you?" Christine asked Tommy.

Tommy nodded. "Guilty. I haven't been out on the water in

a few weeks, and I'm craving it. I even convinced Lola to come along with me."

Lola's eyes brightened. "Christine! You should come with us."

Audrey grumbled from the back. "Don't worry about me. I don't even want to go."

"Next time, baby. When you heal up a little bit more," Lola said tenderly.

Christine turned her eyes out toward the bright Vineyard Sound. She hadn't been off the island, on a boat, in what seemed like forever. The idea of it felt like freedom. Before she knew it, she nodded and said, "Okay. All right. I'll go."

"Really?" Both Lola and Tommy's eyes bugged out of their heads the slightest bit.

Lola gripped Christine's elbow and said, "You're going to love it. I've wanted to take you along for ages. I thought you hated the idea."

Back at the Sheridan house, Lola and Christine got Audrey settled in her bedroom upstairs. Christine noted that the kitchen was crystal clean, to which Lola said, "Amanda is a master at that. I want to hire her for mine and Tommy's place."

"It's not that bad," Tommy stated.

"We can't help it. We're free spirits," Lola teased as she kissed Tommy on the cheek.

The sight made Christine's stomach cramp. For months, she'd had love. Now, she was back to her traditional, Christine ways: alone in the world. No love for her. No romance. That was the stuff other people were allowed to have.

Just as she had the previous week or so, Christine felt pretty helpless as she watched Tommy prepare the sailboat. She and Lola had dressed in multiple layers, so much so that she felt like a blimp, and she huddled out of the way while Tommy sauntered to and fro.

"He's like a master of the seas," Christine said teasingly.

Lola nodded. "You really should have seen him when we encountered that horrible storm last August. I thought we were dead meat. Shark snacks."

Before they'd headed out, they had stopped at the grocery store to pick up some bottles of wine, cheese, crackers, and fruit. Christine held the basket tightly as the sailboat surged out across the waves, abandoning the island. It was a surprise, how freeing it really felt. It was almost as though Christine had left all the darkness behind. Almost.

They sailed for a while without speaking. Christine watched Lola's beautiful hair flip out wildly with the wind. Occasionally, she would watch Lola's eyes turn toward Tommy with love as he opened a sail or tightened one down.

After a while, the sailboat passed by the cliffs along the southwestern tip of the island. Christine removed the bottle of wine from the basket as Lola clapped her gloved hands together and said, "Yes! I think it's time for a toast to Baby Max's progress."

Christine poured them glasses. They lifted them toward the island as Christine announced, "To our dear, sweet Max Sheridan. We love you more than words. And we can't wait to share the waters of the Vineyard Sound with you. I know you'll be just as graceful on the sea as your grandmother's boyfriend."

"A grandmother's boyfriend!" Lola cackled. "I can't believe I'm a grandmother. I'm not even forty yet."

"You always get everything out of the way early," Christine said as she wagged her eyebrows.

Lola jabbed her with her elbow playfully. "I never should have told you when I lost my virginity."

"You were so proud of it! So early! Before any of your friends," Christine replied, cackling.

"She's a wild one," Tommy agreed. "But I wouldn't have it any other way."

Christine allowed the soft red wine to fall across her

tongue. Her eyes swept across the top of the island. "I can't believe it's all there. Our entire life, on top of that big rock. I used to feel like I owned the entire world back when I traveled so much for work. But in reality, I was just a stranger in a strange world."

Lola nodded. "I have asked myself a few times if, in coming here, I gave up on the world. But I don't think so. We can come and go as we please, but we always have a place to call home. Even Tommy, a guy who always said he would never call anywhere home but now gets a tiny bit homesick when he's out on the boat too long. Don't you, Tommy?"

Tommy gave her a look that said he'd asked her to keep that information to herself. At this, both Lola and Christine burst into giggles.

They continued to sail through the glow of the afternoon. They went over the baby's progress again and discussed what would happen if the baby was eventually given over to them.

"I can bring the supplies from the nursery over to the house," Christine said. "Audrey and I both sleep upstairs, so we can create a little baby haven up there."

Lola nodded as she stitched her brows together. Christine could sense her question— one revolving around Zach and if he would ever return home.

At this, Christine shrugged and said, "I don't want to be in that house without him. It's too sad. I just want to be at our family house with everyone else. There's so much love there. I don't want Max to feel any sadness or as though anything is off."

Lola pressed her lips in a straight line as she poured herself another glass. "And you still haven't heard from him?"

"No. Nothing at all." It felt like a punch to the cheek. "And the bistro is like a ghost town."

"Don't worry about the bistro," Lola muttered. "I just can't understand why he would do this. We've all gone through tremendous pain."

"But we've never lost a child," Christine whispered. "At least, not yet."

They dropped their chins low and considered the heaviness of those words. How scary they actually were to even say. Inwardly, Christine cursed herself again for ever thinking she could have the life of her dreams. But at that moment, the sails lifted, the wind rushed through them, and the water smashed against the sides of the glorious boat. She forced her eyes up; she forced herself to see, to truly see what surrounded her.

She had the most beautiful life in the world. She needed to be grateful for it. No matter what happened.

Chapter Thirteen

Audrey hadn't yet made it through an entire night of sleep. Every few hours, her eyes popped open, and her hands went to that once-familiar place, her abdomen, which had started its gradual shrink back toward her hips. There was no baby in there, she reminded herself in the dead of night. Her baby was far away, at the hospital. Her baby was a separate entity, a boy with a brain of his own and ten fingers and ten toes.

At around four in the morning, on March 10 and very nearly two weeks after Max's birth, Audrey appeared downstairs in front of the kitchen table. There, she found her Grandpa Wes alert, his eyes toward the water. He had a pen lifted, the tip of it against one of the boxes of a crossword. Before the birth of Max, Audrey and Grandpa Wes had done a number of crosswords together. They were one of Audrey's favorite pastimes, for one, but for two, she had read that doing puzzles like that helped dementia patients. Day after day, box after box, they'd filled in crosswords. And then, on February

27, Max had been born, and Audrey hadn't bothered with a single crossword since. Actually, she hadn't even thought of it.

"Morning, Grandpa," she said.

Grandpa Wes yanked his head around, surprised. "You know it's only four in the morning, don't you?"

"I do." Audrey stepped into the kitchen area to brew a pot of coffee. She then joined her grandfather at the table and tilted her head to see the clues for the crossword, so tiny and dull with the soft light from the hanging lamp.

"You couldn't sleep either, then?" Audrey finally asked him.

Grandpa Wes removed his glasses and wiped a handkerchief across his forehead. "I had a bad dream. Although for the life of me, I can't remember what it was about now."

"Me too," Audrey told him. She, too, couldn't fully remember the dream, although it had had something to do with Max and her mother, two people on this earth she loved the most. "I hate it when your subconscious plays tricks on you like that."

Audrey poured them both cups of coffee, and they sat in general silence, both of them reading the clues of the crossword over and over again. Occasionally, one of them would say, "What about 'AL FRESCA' for forty-two down?" or "I think fifteen across is 'CALLIOPE.'" But otherwise, they let the sun rise around them without any other words. The puzzle was enough for them.

Christine arrived downstairs just after six-thirty. Amanda entered the kitchen area from her bedroom around seven. Audrey brewed more coffee, and there was discussion about who was up to what over the next hours. Naturally, Audrey wanted to head up to the NICU; Christine decided she would join her. They glanced toward Grandpa Wes, who they always had to "deal with" around this time of the day.

"I'll call Kerry," Grandpa Wes said. "Don't you worry your-selves. She already said she wasn't that busy today."

Once Aunt Kerry arrived, Christine and Audrey jumped into Christine's car and headed off to the hospital. As they drove, Audrey recognized a number of people out on the side-walk for morning jogs or walks. "All winter long, people have been hidden away inside, and now, everyone is out to play," she said, as she lifted a hand to greet several passers-by.

"Spring fever," Christine agreed.

Audrey found herself again outside the glass of the NICU. Max had improved a great deal, so much so that there had been talk about him going home the following week. The idea made her feel panicked. Could she actually care for such a sick baby? Was she actually enough?

Audrey collapsed in the chair next to Christine. Christine had her phone out before her, with what looked like Zach's name on top, as though she planned to message him. Audrey drew her eyes away. She didn't want to be a snoop. She'd already seen too much.

Finally, Christine spoke. Her voice crackled. "I don't know what to do about the bistro. I've talked to Susan about maybe hiring a new chef. I don't necessarily want to give up my posi-tion as head pastry chef and baker, but it's looking more and more likely that that will be the case, especially after you head back to Penn State."

This was a discussion Audrey and Christine hadn't broached since Zach's departure. In fact, Audrey had thought several times it might not be possible that she return to school now. She glanced toward her aunt, whose face looked resolute and sure.

"But you love that job," Audrey said softly.

Christine shrugged lightly. "I told you. I'm going to care for your baby when you head back to school. I'll still work at the bakery and bistro in a way, but I will need help. Four in the morning, every day, isn't going to cut it anymore. Not with Max around."

After a pause, Audrey wrapped her arms around Christine's shoulders and hugged her tight. Christine dropped her chin and squeezed her eyes shut. The sacrifices they'd made for their family were impossible to ignore. Audrey knew they would continue on forever. She'd only just learned it the previous year, but that was the Sheridan way.

After all, hadn't her Grandpa Wes lied about what had happened out on that boat all those years ago in order to save his daughters' opinions of their mother, Anna Sheridan, after her death? He'd sacrificed their love for him in order to save their love for Anna. It was a selfless act that wouldn't be forgotten.

It was just like a Sheridan to do that.

"I have to clear my head," Christine said softly. She rubbed her forehead and then rose up. Audrey's hands fell down to her lap. "Do you need anything while I'm out?"

"I guess I would take a donut from the Frosted Delights," Audrey said. "If you head that way."

"You got it." Christine smiled before walking away.

Audrey sat alone for about twenty minutes after that. She felt a strange moment of pain, but it soon subsided. If there was anything she'd learned from the horrendous, many, many hours of labor, it was that bodies worked in mysterious ways. She'd always been able to trust hers to pull her through until it had betrayed her with Max's birth.

A figure appeared down the long hallway. It approached, but Audrey didn't bother to turn her head that way. Then, there was the clunk-clunk of quarters entering the vending machine. Audrey's eyes twitched just left to find the guy who'd procured her Reese's Pieces the previous week. His smile was mischievous as he slipped his hand through the bottom of the machine and drew out an orange package of her favorite snack.

"What are you doing? Did Reese's Pieces hire you to market their product to me?" Audrey joked. "Tell them they've wasted their money. I'm already a forever customer."

The guy chuckled as he stepped toward her. "Can I sit here?"

Audrey shrugged. "It's a free country, isn't it?"

Was she flirting with him? Was that what this was? She wasn't sure. But she liked how she felt when she spoke to him. She felt like pre-pregnancy Audrey.

The guy ripped open the package of candy and gestured the bag toward her. She splayed out her palm and accepted not just a few but a whole handful of yellow and orange and brown candies.

"You're too generous," she said with a laugh.

"Am I?" He shrugged and then tossed some candies into his mouth. "My mother raised me right, I guess."

Audrey chuckled at the joke, even as his eyes became shadowed. Obviously, the fact that they both remained here, in front of the glass at the NICU, meant that their lives weren't going exactly as planned.

"Is she okay? Your mom?" Audrey asked softly.

The guy shrugged. "She's okay. She's up here a lot, but I made her stay home to get some rest. She hates when Matilda is up here by herself, so here I am."

"Of course," Audrey said.

"What about your mom?" he asked. "Is she okay?"

Audrey nodded. Her cheeks brightened red with the lie. "Just tired. But we have a lot of family to help out with everything. It was hard for her to eat for a while. I think she was just so upset. But she's getting her strength back."

The guy chewed contemplatively. Audrey almost liked that she didn't know his name. She could imagine a few different ones— all names she'd heard at college, stand-ins for the hottest guys on campus. Garret. Rhett. Quintin. But she didn't dare ask him. Somehow, it would break the illusion.

And besides, they couldn't get "real." If they did, she would have to tell him she was the mother, that that baby was her baby. That she was a nineteen-year-old mother and this had all been her big, fat mistake.

"I just don't know how to help her, you know?" the guy said softly.

For the first time, Audrey realized that he was on the verge of crying. He placed the package of candy off to the side and spread his hands out on his thighs. His shoulders shook.

"It's just been mom and me all this time. And when she told me about the baby, I was a bit apprehensive. But it made her so happy, so happy. And now, I don't think I've ever seen her so sad. She needs therapy, but she doesn't want to do anything outside of being here or resting. And I know she blames herself. I keep telling her that she shouldn't, but it's no use."

Audrey placed her hand on the young man's shoulder and then positioned it across his hand. She gripped his palm gently and continued to stare straight ahead. There was so much between them, so much they understood about the other that they didn't even need to say.

Audrey's tears rolled slowly down her cheek. She didn't bother to brush them away. She noticed, after a while, that the guy cried, too. He didn't bother to clean himself up, either. Neither of them spoke for a good twenty minutes. Then, they reached thirty. Audrey wondered if they would remain like that, eyes forward, toward his sister and her son in the NICU, until time itself stopped.

Christine appeared beside them at some point. Audrey blinked up at her, confused, but still with her hand over the stranger's. Christine splayed her hands out on either side of her. It was clear she'd been crying, as her eyes were tinged with red. When she spoke, her voice was all gurgled.

"I forgot the donuts," she said. She looked on the verge of breaking down completely.

Audrey stood, released his hand, and hugged Christine. The guy probably thought that Christine was both her and Max's mother. Audrey didn't bother to correct him.

Audrey walked with Christine outside. They stood out near the docks and watched the sailboats as they shifted lightly in the springtime breeze.

"Who is that young man?" Christine finally asked.

"I don't really know," Audrey returned. She then licked her chapped lips and said, "It's just good to not be alone."

Chapter Fourteen

March 14. How was it possible? Time just ticked away as little Max got stronger; even still, with every passing day, Christine felt more and more proof that she'd lost total grip on her normal life. She still hadn't heard from Zach; she'd hardly been able to head over to the house they'd shared together. Most recently, she'd asked Susan to go with her and then had waited outside while she had filled another suitcase with Christine's clothes.

Christine hovered at the kitchen sink and blinked down at the pile-up of bowls, spoons, plates, and forks. This was an unnatural sight in a kitchen that was normally run like a tight ship by Amanda, but Amanda had left the island the previous afternoon to take care of something at Rutgers, where she continued to take online law school classes.

Christine lifted her phone and texted her niece.

> CHRISTINE: It's funny how this place falls apart without you here.

Amanda texted back just a few seconds later.

AMANDA: I don't know what to do with you guys.

CHRISTINE: Don't worry. I'll keep everything at bay until you get back.

AMANDA: I'll buy extra sponges on my way home.

Christine smiled to herself, heaved a sigh, pulled up her sleeves, and began to scrub the plates and bowls. The hot water was relaxing on her skin, and for a few minutes, she managed to keep the focus on nothing but the milk streaming out of the cereal bowls and the gunk coming off the now-shining plates. Maybe this was why Amanda liked to clean so much. It was an ultimate before-and-after. It was a relief from the messiness of real life.

It wasn't enough to convert Christine into a clean freak, though.

There was the sound of the screen door near the driveway. In a moment, Audrey appeared, leading her grandfather toward the kitchen table. In her arms, she held two paper bags filled with groceries. She stopped short and looked at Christine with wide eyes. "Did you do those dishes?"

Christine laughed. "Yep."

"I got some groceries," Audrey said. "I realized we were out of almost everything. How does Amanda manage to do all this without us noticing?"

"Good question," Christine said.

"The woman has talent. I'll give her that," Audrey said. She slid the two paper bags onto the counter and then turned toward her grandfather. "I don't think we should hide the donuts from Christine. She'll sense them."

Slowly, Wes brought a bag of Frosted Delights donuts out from around his back and placed it alongside the groceries.

Christine laughed again, a true, genuine laugh, and said, "I can't believe you guys wanted to hold out on me."

"You know how Grandpa is. He wants them all for himself." Audrey winked at him.

Hope was a funny thing. It was true what all the poets said: *It gave you wings.*

Together, the three of them sat at the kitchen table and gossiped about people Grandpa Wes and Audrey had seen in town and about how Jennifer Conrad's mother, Ariane, had been at the Frosted Delights Bakery and seemed to be doing better in the wake of her stroke.

"We even spotted Jennifer's new boyfriend," Wes said.

"That's right! He's a hunk," Audrey said decidedly.

That afternoon, Christine, Audrey, and Lola gathered at the doctor's office once more to hear about Baby Max's progress. Lola wore a bohemian dress that whirled around her ankles, with little dark red, sharp-toed boots. Christine thought this was a funny sight, too. Since Max's birth, none of them had bothered much with fashion.

Maybe it was finally time to return to some kind of normality. Maybe it was time to acknowledge beautiful things again.

The doctor explained Max's progress with bright, optimistic eyes. "I think another two or three days of monitoring, and then he'll be ready to go on home."

Audrey slapped her hand across Christine's knee with joy, which made her jump in her chair. Audrey looked like she wanted to jump over the desk and wrap her arms around the doctor. She looked like she could fly to the moon.

Audrey had only been allowed to hold baby Max a few times. The doctor said that today seemed like an appropriate day. Audrey got all dressed up in scrubs, wore a mask, and then followed the doctor into the NICU. Christine and Lola huddled outside the glass for support.

"Look at her," Christine breathed. "She's a total natural,

isn't she? The love she has for that boy is rolling off her in waves."

A tear rolled down Lola's cheek. "I don't know what to say. I'm just so relieved and overjoyed."

Audrey sat with her beautiful baby, and their eyes locked. Christine could already feel the conversations that would flow between mother and son over the years as they grew together in love. It was so strange and so wonderful that Christine would be a part of that. She would know this baby as he grew older. In the beginning, she would be privy to so many, many firsts— his first smile, his first roll-over, his first step, and his first word.

When Lola, Audrey, and Christine stepped out into the bright light of the afternoon, Susan pulled up in her car, rolled down the window, and said, "Fancy seeing you three beauties here."

Christine laughed as they stepped closer. Behind Susan's car, an angry driver blared his horn and then whipped around her. Susan just rolled her eyes and said, "Loosen up. We're on island time, aren't we?"

Audrey told Susan the news of the baby, and Susan lifted her hands to her eyes and exhaled deeply. "That is the best news I've ever heard," she murmured with relief. After a pause, she said, "That's it. We have to have a big, old-fashioned Sheridan dinner. Don't you think?"

The menu was decided in a flurry of words at the grocery store. Christine felt like a little kid again as she, Lola, Audrey, and Susan flung various items into the grocery cart, cracked jokes, and giggled to their hearts' content there in the grocery aisles. One of the grocery store employees gave them the stink eye, which made them laugh even more.

Christine hadn't felt this light, this alive, since Christmas, maybe. Sure, Zach had left; maybe she'd never see him again. But she had her girls, and she had Max. Beyond that, there was nothing a few pints of ice cream couldn't solve. And because the Sheridan girls appreciated the finer things in life, they did, in fact, put a few tubs of Ben and Jerry's in the bottom of the cart.

They invited everyone they could think of. Scott came over and started the grill out on the front porch and came in frequently to sip his beer and warm up and dot little kisses on Susan's cheeks. Tommy arrived at around five-thirty with a twelve-pack of beer, wind-swept hair from a wild trek out on the ocean, and several bags of chips, which they'd apparently forgotten to buy at the grocery store. He clapped Audrey on the shoulder and beamed at her.

"Sounds like you're about to bring your boy home," he said.

Audrey and Christine stood off to the side while various guests arrived. Audrey was strangely quiet, although she beamed at everyone as they entered. Christine, who'd always been more of the surly, depressive one at parties like this, understood her need to be quiet. Obviously, her thoughts were like a tornado.

Scott cooked burgers, sausages, and steaks. One of the tables was filled to the brim with potato salad, sliced fruits, cheese platters, and various types of other finger foods. Aunt Kerry came in with a big pot of soup and placed it on the right-hand side of the table. As a result, the table very nearly tipped over. Tommy whipped across the room and grabbed the corner of the table just in time.

"Wow. Impressive," Lola remarked. She jumped to action as well and placed the soup in the center of the table as Tommy set the base back in a better position. She lifted her chin to kiss him as Aunt Kerry clapped her hands. In the kitchen area, Susan prepared yet another salad as Scott's arms wrapped around her waist from behind and held her close against him, his chin resting on her shoulder. Toward the window, Wes and Trevor stood and ate chips and discussed a recent basketball game. It was March Madness, and apparently, there was a lot to say. This had been completely off of Christine's radar. The passage of time was such a strange thing.

Everywhere Christine looked, there was tremendous love. She ate her burger slowly, then placed it, half-eaten, on her plate. Audrey began to discuss something with Lola about a recent article Lola had to write for the *Tribune*, and Christine was impressed that Audrey could even draw up thoughts that didn't have anything to do with Max.

"When you're back at college, you'll probably have to take a class on the research process," Lola said, her eyebrows lowering. "For any given article, you need at least two or three sources to back up any given claim."

"But how do you even find people to fit the narrative of the story?" Audrey demanded.

"It's a lot of work, my girl," Lola said, her smile widening. "But you'll get it."

At around eight, the screen door pushed open to reveal Amanda. She beamed as she entered and removed her travel backpack from her shoulders. "Thanks for throwing a party without me, guys!" she yelled out playfully. She then threw her arms around Audrey and whispered words just loud enough for Christine to hear. "I can't believe we'll get that baby home with us soon. I'm so glad. My heart is bursting."

Amanda passed by Christine as she headed toward her bedroom. She paused, lifted her hand to Christine's elbow, and made eye contact. Christine was suddenly very aware that she hadn't said a single word in thirty minutes, maybe more. She felt a little awkward.

"Can I talk to you about something?" Amanda said softly.

Christine lifted her glass of wine and followed behind Amanda, wordless. There was an urgency to Amanda's eyes, something that told her the twenty-two-year-old girl meant business.

Once inside Amanda's bedroom, she shut the door closed,

heaved a sigh, and said, "Christine, I just saw Zach."

Christine's heart dropped into her belly. "What? Where?" She barely recognized her own voice.

Amanda shrugged. "I saw his car just outside the driveway. He was inside like he was trying to dare himself to come in. I don't know."

Christine's throat constricted. "I thought he left the Vineyard."

"I guess he's back," Amanda told her, lying her backpack on the edge of the bed.

Christine felt unsure of what to do. "What do you think I should do?" How ridiculous that she asked this question of her twenty-two-year-old niece. Somehow, at this moment, Amanda seemed worlds more mature than her.

"It's up to you," Amanda said softly. "I mean, he really messed up. He like, Chris-style messed up."

"True." Christine couldn't bring herself to smile, even as Amanda picked fun at her own heartache.

"But he did look miserable," Amanda offered. "And he did come back. Chris never did that. I'm sure he has been struggling with his own demons, his past."

Christine walked in slow-motion. She felt herself go into the back mudroom, reach for her coat, and place her hat on her head. It was the middle of March, but when the sun sank below the horizon line, that same winter chill took over the air. Before anyone could ask her what she was up to, she walked out onto the back porch and then walked toward the main road. The moon cast a strange light over everything. She felt as though she had walked through a dream.

When she reached the main road, she turned left to find Zach at the steering wheel of his car. He looked at her like a deer in headlights. She remained in front of him, with her hands pushed deep in her coat pocket. Slowly, he opened the car door and stepped out into the chilly air. They were about ten feet apart from each other, which was the closest they'd been since he had bailed on her weeks before.

The silence stretched between them ominously. They locked eyes, as though each of them dared the other to speak first. Christine had never thought of herself as "brave," exactly. But she just couldn't bear the stillness any longer.

"I'm glad you're all right," she finally said.

Zach's eyes dropped to the ground. He looked so sheepish and so sorry.

"I don't know what to say," Zach muttered.

Christine had about a million responses to that. *You should have stayed. You should have been here to support Audrey and me. You should have done what you promised to do.*

But she couldn't bring herself to say any of it.

"I think you should go," Christine finally said. She crossed her arms over her chest; she built a wall between them.

Zach brought his eyes back toward hers. "Will you please let me explain?"

Christine bit her lip for a long moment. Then, she said, "I don't know if you deserve that after what you did."

Zach sucked his cheeks in. Christine felt like she'd just smacked him across the face, even though they were still ten feet from one another. Every single piece of her soul told her to jump toward him and wrap her arms around him. She wanted to sob against his chest. She needed him so badly.

But she couldn't let herself give in. He'd proved himself to not be loyal, unable to care for her and the baby and Audrey. *What would happen if another serious issue arose? Would he just run off again?*

Finally, Zach dropped back into the car. He nodded and then pulled the car door back in place. Christine turned back toward the house and walked slowly, somberly. There was the sound of the engine, then the creak of the tires. In a moment, he was gone for good.

Chapter Fifteen

"*You're a monster, Christine. You bring all this bad luck on yourself. You can't blame anyone else.*"

The words rang through Christine's head late at night. She tossed and turned in the upstairs bedroom as sweat ran down her lower back and across her upper lip. She closed her eyes to try to drive out the thoughts, but they came back even stronger.

"*You can't think that I make you drink like you do, Christine. You're trying to run from something. But it isn't me you're trying to run from. You're running from yourself.*"

Christine's eyes popped open again. She turned to face the moon, which hovered like a strange creep out the window. The words weren't exactly what her ex-boyfriend had said up in New York; they were like a mix of all the insults that previous ex-boyfriends had flung her way through her strange, twenty-year stint as a single woman in the world.

Now, she had pushed the only man she'd ever really loved away when he'd come back to try to explain himself.

But she was tired of being knocked around. *Why was Susan*

allowed such a beautiful, honest, and open relationship with Scott? Why was Lola allowed adventure and beauty with Tommy? Where was Christine's happy ending? Why did it happen for everyone else?

Christine checked her phone. It was three in the morning. In a previous era, she might have forced herself awake at this point, as she normally liked to be at the bakery around four or four-thirty. She had never even really questioned that early wake-up time. She'd craved it: the silence of the mornings, the darkness outside the window as she preheated the ovens, the feel of the dough beneath her fingers. During those moments, she was allowed complete solitude. And in that silence, she felt free.

Before she knew what she was doing, Christine whipped the blankets from her legs and stepped out into the chilly air. She jumped into the shower, scrubbed herself clean, and dried her hair, all without thinking another thought. By the time she snapped the lights on at the bistro itself, her eyes were wide open, and her heart felt full.

If she wanted to bake, then by gosh, she would bake.

It was strange, knowing that nobody would arrive in the next few hours to set up the bistro for breakfast service. As Christine set to work on the croissants, the banana bread, the sourdough bread, and a few batches of cookies, she played music to drown out her thoughts. Each of the albums she picked were reflections of previous times in her life. She remembered her obsession with Patti Smith, age twenty-two, one of the years she'd perfected crème brûlée. She then thought back to her late twenties, when she'd loved party music and had taken to the many clubs of Manhattan with zeal. She danced around the kitchen as she stirred, baked, and lost herself in time.

Of course, every hour or so, the same thought returned to her: *What the heck is wrong with me?*

She had always wondered this. As a teenager, she'd been the odd one out, while Susan had been the goody-two-shoes, and Lola had been the "wild, adventurous one." Christine Sheridan? She was dark. Mysterious. Don't get too close to her.

"I should have known it wasn't going to work," Christine breathed.

She stepped toward the oven around daybreak to peer in. The croissants rounded beautifully beneath the orange light. According to Susan, the inn was pretty full, despite the chill that remained in the air. She knew the guests would bite, especially if she set up a little table near the front desk. If she didn't sell out, the croissants didn't have a long shelf-life, anyway. The Sheridans were eaters, and front-desk Sam was in his mid-twenties and, therefore, a bottomless pit.

Christine noticed that Zach's office door was slightly ajar. She stepped toward it and pushed it open further. With the light cast over the space from the kitchen, she could make out the swivel chair, the massive desk, and the framed photograph of Christine and Zach from a long-lost day in early autumn when they had gone hiking along the coastline. Christine could see it in her expression: she had her eyes closed and her lips pressed against his cheek, and she loved him more than life itself. Zach's expression was euphoric, as though he'd just learned he'd won the lottery.

Wow. They'd really messed up a good thing, hadn't they?

Christine stepped into the office and perched at the edge of Zach's chair. On the coat hanger to the left of the desk hung two of Zach's winter hats, along with a sweater with a big ketchup stain on the back. Christine had been there for that incident, too. They had eaten French fries together between lunch and dinner rushes while making fun of some of their more annoying customers. *"They don't understand your genius,"* Christine had said with a laugh. *"You're an artist. Not just a cook."* Knowing she teased him, Zach had drawn his arm around her neck, as a boxer might, and said, *"Don't you dare make fun of me, Christine Sheridan!"* Around then, he had accidentally knocked the ketchup over, and that had been it. They'd burst into endless laughter.

Once the croissants were finished, Christine took a whole batch out toward the front desk. Susan and Sam stood behind it and analyzed a number of official-looking documents. Again, Christine thanked her lucky stars that she wasn't involved in some of the intricate parts of the Sunrise Cove.

"Christine Sheridan! What are you doing here?" Susan asked. Her smile was electric.

Christine lifted the tray of croissants. She felt like a pastry graduate showing off her baking skills. "I just felt like baking today, I guess."

But neither Sam nor Susan made her feel anything but warmth. Sam wolfed down three croissants without even thinking about it, and Susan said they were even better than she'd remembered.

"I thought we could sell some to the guests," Christine suggested. "Maybe set up a little table right here by the front desk?"

Sam set to work. He prepared a table then positioned the croissants, some banana bread, sourdough, and other delicacies on various brightly-colored dishes. He looked focused, his eyebrows low, and Christine sat back and leaned against the counter. The exhaustion from not sleeping and baking all morning hit her like a punch to the face.

"You okay?" Susan asked under her breath.

Christine buzzed her lips. "Depends on the meaning of okay."

Susan squeezed Christine's upper arm. "Amanda might have mentioned that Zach stopped by the house last night."

Christine should have known that Amanda would fess up to her mother. They were thicker than thieves, those two.

"He did, yeah."

"What happened?"

Christine squeezed her eyes shut, a failed attempt to keep from crying all over again. "He wanted to explain why he just up and disappeared, but I wouldn't let him."

There was silence for a moment. Finally, Susan replied, "It makes sense. He messed up. Bad."

Christine's shoulders shook. "I just wanted us to work out so much. I don't know why he had to do this. We had such a good thing going."

Susan's hand rubbed the apex of Christine's back and slowly eased over her shoulder. Christine knew her body was tight as ever; she was in real need of a massage or some kind of hug, but she hadn't gone out of her way to get it. Everyone was focused on baby Max— including herself. She didn't need anyone, or so she thought.

"What do you think?" Sam called from the table. He gestured toward the croissants and the cookies.

"Great display," Christine remarked, although she could hardly see it through her tears. "If you build it, they will come."

A few minutes later, Sam went upstairs to tend to another guest. Christine turned and leaned on her elbows while Susan made several notes to herself on a notepad. She muttered as she wrote, something she'd done ever since she'd been a little girl. Christine wanted to point this out, but she held it back. Maybe Susan didn't even know she did it.

"I want to discuss something with you, Christine," Susan said then. She bit on her lower lip and then turned her eyes upward, but they didn't meet Christine's.

Christine's heart thudded strangely. "Okay."

"Now that things are slowing down, and Max will be coming home, we need to find a way back to normality," Susan continued.

"I agree," Christine said, although she wasn't fully sure what Susan meant.

"I hate to say it, but the guests need a place to eat. And we're losing a lot of revenue with the bistro closed," Susan continued.

Christine's throat was filled with lumps. She nodded somberly, as though she totally agreed.

"And I was considering finally putting up an ad for a new chef position," Susan went on. "But I wanted to tell you before I made it official.."

Christine wanted to scream into the abyss. She wanted to yell and scream that things should have been different. For a long time, she let the silence between herself and her sister fester. And then, after another pause, she nodded somberly.

"Of course. The bistro needs to be open. I think we can all agree on that."

Susan exhaled deeply. "I'm so glad to hear you say that. I was so worried. But I really need your help in picking out someone perfect for the place. You know the restaurant world better than anyone."

"True. I do," Christine said sadly.

"Maybe we can find a really wonderful female chef," Susan suggested brightly.

Christine knew that Susan meant only the best with this sentiment. Still, it felt like just another slap in the face, like Christine just couldn't handle having a man around, or else she would get sexually involved with him. It was, after all, her typical story.

Gosh, what was wrong with her?

"Yeah. A female chef," Christine said. Her bright voice sounded like it belonged to someone else.

"Anyway. I have to run," Susan said. "Amanda is waiting for me at the office. We have about three meetings lined up this morning, if you can believe it. Do you mind standing at this desk for a few minutes until Sam gets back? I'm sure he won't be long."

Christine found herself behind the front desk with her arms hanging sadly at her sides. She was hardly aware of anything around her. In a weird way, she cursed the exterior weather, the way spring had flung itself over everything, as though flaunting the passage of time in her face. Give her anything else! Give her winter if it meant it was the previous one before all had gone wrong in her world.

A woman in her late sixties appeared at the front desk a few minutes later. It took Christine a few moments to even recognized that the woman needed something from her. She wore only a robe and a pair of slippers, and her dyed red curls were lined with white.

"Hello? Can you please get me a spare towel?" the woman asked. Her voice was clearly annoyed at this point, which meant that she'd asked already a few times, and Christine just hadn't noticed.

"A new towel?" Christine asked. The words sounded foreign. With a jolt, she realized she hardly knew where they kept anything like that these days. "Of course. I can. Um. Let's go find one."

Christine led the woman down the back hallway, where she tried the first closet, then the next, until she traipsed her back up the hallway toward the staircase. The woman grumbled to herself as they went, but Christine was too exhausted to explain herself.

Upstairs, Christine opened yet another closet and found only cleaning supplies and unused sponges piled up. Immediately, she burst into tears. Her body shook with panic and sadness and fear. It was the culmination of everything, but it happened here, in front of this woman. How embarrassing.

The woman's eyebrows raised high on her forehead. For a

long time, she gazed at Christine, who really couldn't get ahold of herself.

After another few of Christine's sobs echoed through the hallway, the woman said, "You know, it's really just a towel. I can probably do without it." Then, she disappeared down the hallway and out of sight.

Chapter Sixteen

March 17. It was St. Patrick's Day, a full nineteen days after Max's birth, and Audrey again awoke before the crack of dawn, prepared a pot of coffee, and gazed out across the horizon line, in wait for that first peek of gray light. Today was the day she would bring her baby home. Today was the day everything would change for good, and she was allowed to test herself at being a mother. She was crawling out of her skin.

The previous afternoon, Audrey and Lola had stopped by Christine and Zach's place to pick up all the baby supplies. Christine had given them the key, along with instructions on where everything was, and Audrey and Lola had gone, alert, big-eyed, fully aware that they might have a Zach interaction once there. But when they entered, he was nowhere to be found. The place was spick-and-span. Much cleaner than Audrey had seen it when Christine had lived there with Zach. Lola had snuck a peek in the fridge to find a full selection of fruits, vegetables, and deli meats.

"Looks like someone's on a health kick," Lola had said with her eyebrows raised.

"He's not cooking," Audrey had said, surprised. "I've never seen Zach eat a sandwich before. He's always cooking up some weird gourmet meal."

"True," Lola had said. "I wonder where he is. And I wonder how long his money will hold out. Maybe he came to talk to Christine the other night because he realized he needed his job back? He needed to get back with her so he could get it?"

Audrey hadn't wanted to think so poorly of Zach, at least, not yet. "He loves her, I believe. He just got scared."

Lola had sniffed. "I don't know. The world can be really cruel, Audrey."

"You're talking to a girl who just gave birth to a really sick baby without his father around," Audrey had returned. "Don't tell me the world can be cruel."

"Good point," Lola had replied.

But now that they had gone through the nursery and brought all the supplies to the Sheridan house, they'd set up a little nursery area in one of the bedrooms upstairs. Looking at it there, the crib and the little bear decorations and the stuffed animals, had sent Audrey into a kind of spiral. She'd done it; she had given birth. Maybe all would be okay. But was it too soon to think it would be?

Lola had told her that once you were a mother, you never stopped worrying. When you brought a child into the world, you were changed forever. Audrey now knew that first-hand.

"There she is." Grandpa Wes opened the door of his bedroom and grinned through the haze of the morning light. He wore only a pair of sweatpants, and his belly, normally hidden by a big sweater, protruded.

Audrey giggled. "Where's your shirt, old man?"

Grandpa Wes chuckled as he smacked his stomach. "I gotta lay off the croissants, don't I?"

"We all do," Audrey said. She turned to show him her stomach, which still protruded a bit, nearly three weeks after Max's birth.

"You'll be back to normal in no time," Grandpa Wes told her with a wink.

"Not with Christine's baking frenzies happening around us," Audrey said. "It's her way of nesting for the baby; I get that. I have to latch onto Amanda and start going to the gym after I'm cleared to exercise, I guess. Grandpa, I've literally never excrcised a single day in my life."

Grandpa Wes opened the cookie jar, snaked a hand in, and grabbed a chocolate chip cookie. "Neither have I," he said, flashing her a devilish grin.

"Cookies for breakfast?" Audrey imitated an old commercial she remembered from childhood. She then stepped toward the jar and grabbed her own. "You know, we can never tell Amanda we do stuff like this. She'll never approve."

"Oh, I know," Grandpa Wes said. "She's just like Susan."

"And me? Just like Lola?"

Grandpa Wes arched an cyebrow contemplatively. "I used to think so, Aud. But now, I think I see you as this whole other creature. You're smart and savvy and funny like your mother. But you're something else, too. I can't quite put my finger on it."

As he spoke these endearing words, a tiny bit of chocolate melted across his lower lip. Audrey chuckled and handed him a napkin. "I hope it's a compliment, I guess."

"It is," Grandpa Wes told her. "I only wish your grandmother knew you. I could see the two of you getting on like gangbusters. Probably, you'd laugh yourselves silly."

Max was to be released at ten-thirty on the dot. For whatever reason, Audrey dressed in one of her nicer dresses, a dark green number, something she'd bought for a fraternity dinner date during her freshman year at Penn State. She remembered her date saying she was "mega hot" at the time; now, when she looked in the mirror, she was just grateful the skirt extended out over the belly and highlighted her slight features above. Her face was tired, but her eyes seemed serene.

For the first time in a long time, she checked herself and decided that no. She didn't miss college at all. Right now, all this was so much better.

Up at the hospital, Christine, Lola, Susan, and Amanda met her outside on the sidewalk, beneath a ridiculously bright mid-March sun. It made Audrey shiver to realize that her son had never been outside in his life. Nearly three weeks on this earth, and all he knew was the NICU. It had to be a perfect first day.

"Someone dressed for St. Patrick's Day," Susan said. Her eyes skated down Audrey's dress.

"I need all the luck I can get," Audrey returned. "If the Irish can throw some my way, all the better."

Several minutes before Max's release, Audrey found herself directly next to Christine, who seemed somber and dark and reflective. Behind them, Susan, Amanda, and Lola chatted quietly about something to do with Claire's husband, Russell, and his coming to terms with the city council trying to throw him under the bus.

Finally, Christine exhaled. "I just still can't believe you were there. And you saw all his food in the fridge. And he's still around. But I just don't know what he's up to or what he's thinking or..."

Audrey met Christine's gaze. In her eyes, she saw everything: all the pain and torment of the previous few weeks.

"And Susan is already talking about hiring a new cook. It's like the whole world will just move on," Christine said softly. "And I know in my heart it's a good thing. Look at us now. We're here. We're going to get Max and bring him home. It's one of the happiest days of my life."

Audrey wrapped her arms around Christine and pressed her cheek against her chest. She could feel the thud-thud of Christine's heart. It was safe, this sound. She knew her baby would hear it every day and every night as he fell asleep in Christine's arms while she was gone.

When their hug broke, Christine gripped her hand and said, "But I'm still in this, you know. I'm in this all the way."

"I know," Audrey murmured. Her lower lip quivered with sadness. "I know you won't let us down."

When they released Max, Audrey held him in her arms outside the NICU and gazed down at his perfect little face, the glow of his cheeks, his little button nose, and the tender, soft skin of his ten toes as they bobbed around. His eyes were bright blue, and his nose twitched slightly as he tried to focus on his mother's face. Their eyes locked as Audrey's heart tightened.

"Hello Max, my beautiful, perfect little boy," she whispered to him. "We're going to take you home."

"He looks so strong, doesn't he?" Lola said. She lifted a hand to his toe and wiggled it just the slightest bit. "We have such a little boy to dote on, don't we?"

"Remember how much you wanted a girl?" Susan asked, looking between Audrey and Max.

Audrey laughed. "I honestly barely remember that. It feels like that was someone else."

It took forever for Audrey to wrap up the baby in winter clothing. She insisted that she do it herself since she had to learn sometime, although, of course, Lola and Susan hovered over her and gave her instructions as she went. Audrey wanted to be delicate with the baby in all things, but Aunt Susan told her that babies don't break, that they can handle much more than the layperson thought. This was something Audrey would get used to, she guessed.

When Audrey had Max all dressed up, she placed him in

the baby carriage, turned back, and found herself locking eyes with a familiar man.

There, just a few feet away, stood the stranger from the NICU. The guy who had shared his Reese's Pieces. The guy she'd shared such intimate moments with, without actually knowing his name at all.

"Hi!" Audrey said suddenly.

The guy's smile was warm. He stepped closer and ruffled his hair, proof, maybe, that he was nervous.

Susan, Lola, Amanda, and Christine all eyed him suspiciously. But before they could say anything, the guy said, "I guess I won't see you up here any longer, huh?"

Audrey shook her head. "We're taking him home."

"That is such good news. Congratulations." He turned his eyes toward the woman behind her. He obviously thought one of them was Max's mother.

"And how is your sister?" Audrey asked softly.

"She is doing a lot better. They said maybe another four or five days. We can't wait to bring her home."

Behind her, Christine, Amanda, Lola, and Susan began to discuss what to do about tomorrow's planned "Welcome Home, Max!" party. Christine suggested chili; Susan said they couldn't, as it might hurt Aunt Kerry's feelings that they don't opt for clam chowder. Lola said she didn't care what they ate, as long as there was cake.

Now, this guy and Audrey had space to really talk, as her aunts and mother weren't listening in.

"It was really wonderful to meet you, by the way," Audrey said.

"You too," the guy said.

"Although I have to admit, I have no idea what your name is." Audrey laughed lightly.

"Right. We should have a formal introduction," he said. He stuck his hand out for her to shake. "My name is Noah."

The name smacked Audrey in the heart. It felt like the perfect name for such a handsome, kind, considerate man.

"I'm Audrey," she said as she shook his hand. Their eyes held one another's, just as Max let out the slightest of whimpers.

"Sounds like someone wants to say hi to me, too," Noah said.

Audrey curled her hair behind her ear and blushed. "About that." She turned the buggy to face Noah, took a deep breath, and then said, "Noah, meet Max. This is my son."

Audrey wasn't sure what she'd expected as a response. Maybe she'd expected disgust or shock to play out across his face, something that proved to her just how irresponsible it was to be a young mother.

But instead, Noah crouched down and said, "I am so glad to hear you're well, Max. You have a wonderful mother. She sat outside the glass and watched you as you slept and got better and stronger, day after day. You're one of the lucky ones, Max. Don't you ever forget it."

Audrey's eyes filled with tears. She willed herself not to cry and blinked them back as fast as she could.

When Noah lifted back up to face her, he just nodded. "You're much braver than I thought."

Audrey's cheeks burned bright pink. "Not brave. It just happens to you, I think. When you become a mother."

Neither of them spoke for a moment, not until Max cooed again, and Lola said, "We'd better get him home, Aud."

"Thanks for everything," Audrey told him. "And give your best to your mother and your sister. Tell them both to keep fighting."

"Thank you," he said softly. "That means a lot."

Chapter Seventeen

Max was an inquisitive little baby. On the drive back to the Sheridan house, Audrey tried to match his gaze as he turned his blue eyes left and right. Could his little mind make sense of the trees outside, of the blue rush of the sky, and the billowing clouds? Did he know that this place, Martha's Vineyard, his home, was one of the most beautiful places in the world?

They'd positioned his car seat in the center of the backseat. Christine and Audrey sat on either side of him, captivated, not saying a word. They'd decided to drive back together so that they could all introduce Max to his Great-Grandpa Wes.

Aunt Kerry was over, stirring up a big pot of carrot soup. She beamed at Audrey as she entered with the slumbering baby. Audrey felt as though she carried something breakable, and she walked softly, on only her toes. Grandpa Wes sat on the couch overlooking the water. There, just outside the window, sat a perfect, bright red cardinal. He was captivated.

"Grandpa," Audrey breathed.

There are moments in life that are pure magic. Audrey had

learned this long ago— on the day of her first kiss back in middle school, when the boy she liked more than anyone in the world asked her to prom, or when she'd gotten the internship of her dreams in Chicago. They were moments when the world shifted on its axis, time seemed to stand still, and the air tasted a little brighter. They were moments when you could pretend that everything would be all right, forever.

This was one of those moments.

"What do you have there?" Grandpa Wes asked. His eyes turned to the baby carrier as his hand stretched over his heart.

Audrey had told him the baby would come home that day. It was possible he'd forgotten.

"What do you have there?" he repeated, as his eyes went wide and began to water.

"I have someone who really wants to meet you," Audrey murmured, her voice quivering just the slightest.

Max was fast asleep. His face was perfect, with his lips sitting in a lopsided grin like he was having the most incredible dream. As Audrey positioned him in Grandpa Wes's arms, she watched as a lone tear rolled down her grandfather's cheek. For a long moment, watching the two very separate generations of Sheridan men was priceless.

And then, Grandpa Wes spoke.

"Aren't you a handsome Sheridan man," he said, speaking softly.

Audrey very nearly burst into tears. Grandpa Wes looked like a complete natural with that baby in his arms. For a strange moment, Audrey felt she could see every single era of Wes Sheridan as he'd raised his daughters from birth through their teenage years. How strange that that had been the same man.

He probably hadn't held a baby since then.

Grandpa Wes couldn't take his eyes off of him. In the meantime, Susan stepped into the kitchen and asked Aunt Kerry if she wouldn't mind supplying the clam chowder for the

"Welcome Home, Max" party the following day. Aunt Kerry, as usual, blushed with joy at the idea of being so useful. She also added, "Claire is already bringing a variety of flowers. She's gone a bit crazy with it, in fact."

"No such thing as too many flowers tomorrow, Aunt Kerry," Christine said. She placed her purse on the kitchen table, her eyes still on Max. "Look at how sweet he is. I just can't imagine that he'll ever do anything like cry or keep us up all night or fight with us about curfew."

* * *

These were, of course, famous last words. Baby Max learned how to roar that night, while Christine and Audrey stayed up late to calm him. When they got him to sleep again, Audrey and Christine stood and stared at him for a long time, as though just the idea of crawling back into bed would make him wake again. Neither of them minded. Their world was tied up in his face.

"I really can't imagine going back to college now," Audrey confessed as quietly as she could.

Christine gave her a side-glance. Audrey couldn't read her expression.

Finally, Christine said, "You should do whatever you need to do. Whatever happens, I'll be here. I'll give him whatever he needs."

Audrey dropped her head onto Christine's shoulder. She realized that recently, she hadn't really regarded Christine as an "aunt." She was much closer, somehow. She felt more like a friend. She supposed this was tied up in the fact that she was just as lost as Audrey was, in a way. They were charting their own course in this strange life. They'd never done anything the right way.

Finally, Audrey did make her way back into bed as Christine returned to her bedroom down the hall. Her eyes continued to bore through the darkness, and her ears craned for any sign of Max waking. Once, at around four in the morning, she slowly crawled out of bed again and gazed at him, asleep there in his crib. It was unbelievable to her that she had created something so perfect, so special within her. How was it possible? If anything, she regarded it as a miracle.

The "Welcome Home, Max" party was set to begin the next day, just after one-thirty. When Audrey came downstairs with the baby carrier, she found everyone in the first stages of decoration and preparation. Aunt Kerry stewed up a large pot of clam chowder while Scott sat outside, prepping the grill for later. Susan sat with a wedding magazine on her lap, a fresh one, as Audrey and Amanda had thrown out all the ones from Amanda's wedding planning. Amanda sat beside her and pointed out various elements from the page she liked for Susan's upcoming wedding to Scott on June 19.

"Good morning," Audrey said sweetly as she carried Max toward the kitchen table and placed his baby carrier in the very center. Worry overtook her, and she clutched the edge of the carrier as he slept on.

"Do you want a cup of coffee, Mama?" Lola asked her daughter from the kitchen. She beamed at her through the little window between the kitchen and the table.

"Yes," Audrey said quietly. "More than anything."

"How many times did you get up?" Susan asked as she dropped her magazine to her lap.

"Only once," Audrey replied. "I read that most newborns sleep around sixteen to eighteen hours a day."

"You're right. They do, so enjoy it while you can. I think to be a new mom, you need to have a little bit of blind optimism," Susan said.

The guests began to arrive later on. Andy came in with Will flung over his shoulder as he cackled with delight. Beth scurried in after them, making sure Andy didn't drop Will to the ground.

"I don't know what to do with them," Beth said with a funny sigh.

"Mom! Relax!" Will cried.

Then, there was Kelli and her children, along with Steven and his family. Next came Claire and Charlotte, each carrying countless bouquets of flowers, along with a banner that read, "WELCOME HOME, MAXWELL WESLEY SHERIDAN." Behind them came Claire's husband, Russell, their twin daughters, Rachel, and of course, Everett, who was fresh-faced and handsome as ever. He never looked particularly like "one of the Vineyard men," which was a funny thing. He had this other type of look to him, similar to Tommy.

Tommy had worked his way already out to the grill to operate the burger regime with Scott. Audrey watched Christine's eyes as they scanned toward the men outside. There was a tinge of regret on her face. Obviously, she wanted Zach to be out there with them. *It just wasn't fair, was it?*

Family members approached Audrey and the baby throughout the party. As though to prove her research true, baby Max slept like a rock the entire day. He sat in his little carrier and, every now and then, opened his beautiful blues eyes and let out the cutest little yawn. When someone noticed, it was announced that he was awake, but the moment everyone turned to look, he would fall back asleep. Everyone remarked that he was the most gorgeous baby they'd ever seen— that his face should be on all of the Gerber baby products. Audrey knew people were being overly nice, but she just took it in stride because, after all, this was her son and to her, Max was all that and more.

Amanda dropped to a squat alongside the baby and lifted her finger to his little toe. "You did it, Aud. You created a perfect specimen."

"You will, too. Someday," Audrey told her.

Amanda scoffed. "Yeah, right. I think I lost my chance."

As if on cue, Sam from the Sunrise Cove walked in through the back door, lifted a bottle of wine, and waved it in greeting toward Amanda. Amanda burst to her feet and rushed toward him. "Sam! I thought you said you couldn't make it."

Susan interjected to say, "I told him he had to stop by. If he works at the Sunrise Cove, he's family, isn't he?"

"Yeah, right," Audrey muttered under her breath. "You lost your chance." She rolled her eyes as Amanda began to ask Sam about a recent television show they were both obsessed with, along with questions about an article she had sent him from *The New Yorker*.

It was sickly sweet, their budding friendship-romance. But of course, Audrey was happy for Amanda. She couldn't be all work, all clean-the-house, all-list, and no play. Not forever, anyway.

When Max began to whimper a bit later in the day, Christine approached and asked if she could take him. Exhausted, Audrey nodded and placed him in Christine's arms. She cradled him gently, like a natural, and took him toward Amanda's bedroom with a bottle. Once there, she bobbed him gently as she fed him. Audrey saw her only through the small crack in the door.

Christine's face looked remarkably sad. Audrey had never seen her look like that before. It reflected a love for the baby, of course, but it also told a story about loss and fear and regret. For the first time, Audrey realized the true depths of what Christine was about to do for her if she really went back to Penn State.

She would help raise Audrey's baby.

And then, when Audrey was ready, she would come and take her baby away again.

Christine would be left alone, without Zach, without a baby, and without a love to call her own.

The thought curled itself around Audrey's neck and threatened to strangle her. How she wished everything could be different for Christine.

But just as the thought passed through her, baby Max kicked up one of his beautiful feet, and Christine cupped the foot with a tender hand. She buzzed her lips toward Max's little face, and Max's eyes glinted with joy and, if possible, a new love— a love without judgment.

Chapter Eighteen

March 27.

Audrey hovered above her sleeping babe as the sunlight seeped through the downstairs drapes and cast a shard of brightness across his toes. It was just past seven in the morning, a full month after Max Wesley's birth. Outside, springtime birds tweeted brightly and dug their beaks into the various bird feeds that Audrey and Grandpa Wes had set up only a few days before.

Grandpa Wes stood at the glass with a mug of coffee in hand. He spoke tenderly as he gazed at the birds. "Most of them won't be back till April gets in full swing. But look at this little girl— a Baltimore Oriole. Audrey, have you ever seen anything more beautiful? Oh, and look!" He nearly jumped from his skin. A droplet of coffee came out of the mug and browned his hand. "There, near the dock. I think, if I'm not mistaken, that bright blue ball of energy is an Indigo Bunting."

Audrey lifted baby Max into her arms and stood alongside her grandfather. The flurry of activity from the birds felt necessary and good. As they ate, they shook their heads around and gazed at the wide world around them.

"Where have you been all this time?" Audrey asked them as if they could understand. "The Vineyard missed you."

Amanda walked into the kitchen area. Her hair was messed up, and she still wore pajama pants and a tank top. The noise of her caused two of the birds to flit away from the window.

"Good morning, sunshine." Audrey beamed at her half-asleep cousin.

"I'm late. I'm late?" Amanda said it as though she'd never heard of the concept before. She then walked up the staircase. In a moment, there was the sound of the shower water smashing against the base of the bathtub.

"Did Christine head off to the bistro?" Grandpa Wes asked as he and Audrey shared a laugh.

"I believe so," Audrey replied. "I think I'll head up that way. Maybe take a walk along the docks. Sit in the sun some-where. As long as he's bundled up, he seems happy to be outside."

"No use keeping him cooped up in here," Grandpa Wes agreed.

"And you?" Audrey asked.

"Kerry's coming to pick me up in just a little while. She said she'd cook me pancakes. After that, we'll head out for a walk. I'm sure by that point, Trevor will have picked one topic or another to talk my ear off with," Grandpa Wes said.

Audrey giggled. "You love it."

"True. I'll just serve him right back with all my bird knowledge."

"That'll show him," Audrey said.

Audrey waited for Aunt Kerry to pick up Grandpa Wes before she fully prepared to head out. It was strange, in those moments, as she and her son were the only beings at the normally-full Sheridan house. The big house creaked around them with the springtime breeze. She lifted a baby shoe from the shoe rack and slowly placed it over Max's right foot as he kicked the other playfully. He blinked those big blue eyes at her from over his pacifier. It almost seemed like he knew they were on their way to an adventure. At least a baby-sized adventure.

The sun was like medicine. Audrey pressed the stroller forward as she walked toward town with her cheeks lifted toward it. Everything smelled of fresh blooms and greenery, and she reveled in it. When she reached the Sunrise Cove, Christine stood out front in her baker's apron, her hands on her hips, and her face also lifted toward the sun. Her eyes were closed until she heard the sound of the stroller.

"Audrey! Max!" Christine beamed. She jumped toward them and leaned down to look at Max. "Good morning, little man. Happy one-month birthday. You did it!"

Max cooed appreciatively and then started to nod off.

"How's it going? You've probably been awake for hours," Audrey said.

"Yes. I have. But it's been good. I opened the little window outside the bistro, and plenty of people have come over to buy baked bread and croissants. Apparently, Sam said I'd have it open on our social media. I barely knew we had social media for this old place," Christine admitted.

"I guess the Sunrise Cove has officially entered the twenty-first century," Audrey replied.

Christine brought out some croissants with butter and orange marmalade, which Audrey ate heartily. They spoke about the upcoming doctor's appointment for the baby, which would happen in a few days, along with Audrey's twentieth birthday, on April 7.

"We have to do something special," Christine insisted. "It's your first birthday as a new mom. And you've been through a lot this year."

"To think, just a year ago, I turned nineteen and made out

with a guy at a frat house," Audrey said with a sigh. "My, how the mighty have fallen."

"Come on. If you met that version of yourself, you would laugh at her," Christine said, playfully swatting her hand.

"I would certainly laugh at her slender waistline," Audrey said. She tapped at her belly, which still felt like a bowl of jelly. "I can't wait till I'm cleared to exercise."

"Yeah. We all know how that will work out," Christine said.

Audrey continued on from the Sunrise Cove. She walked with her eyes toward the water as the sunlight played out, dancing along the waves. She thought of future summers when she and Max would romp and play along the beach. She imagined them building a huge sandcastle and sitting inside of it as the waves crashed to shore just beyond. She imagined them becoming best friends like Audrey and Lola had always been. She imagined him telling her his deepest, darkest fears and how grateful she would be that he trusted her enough to give her that. It was such a rare thing to trust anyone in this world.

Audrey was so lost in thought that she nearly stumbled directly into an approaching walker near the docks. When she jumped back, she jerked the stroller, waking Max up slightly.

But the man before her wouldn't budge. It was like he'd wanted to get her attention.

And in a moment, Audrey understood why.

The man who stood, blocking her and Max's path, was Zach Walters.

He looked a bit strange. His cheeks were hollowed out; he had a shaggy, dark blond beard; and he wore clothes Audrey had never seen him in, dark blue sweatpants and a big, baggy sweatshirt. He looked like a guy going through a nervous breakdown of sorts. Even his eyes, normally so alive, looked far away and lost.

"Zach," Audrey breathed.

"Wow. Audrey." He sounded so wistful. His eyes turned toward the baby and immediately glistened. He stared at Max for a long time. It was like he'd forgotten how to speak.

Audrey stepped around to the side of the stroller and adjusted the blanket over Max's little body. "This is Max," she said. Her voice cracked. "Today is his one-month birthday."

"You don't say," Zach whispered, completely mystified. "A whole month."

They stood in silence for a moment. Zach seemed to not be able to get enough of looking at the baby. It was heartbreaking. Zach had wanted to be Max's stand-in father. Now, he was a stranger on the sidewalk.

"Remember all those times," Zach said as he lifted his eyes again. "All those times you were so sure your baby was going to be a girl."

Audrey laughed, surprising herself. In actuality, she'd again completely forgotten about that. The only real reminder was the bright pink blanket, which Aunt Kerry had crocheted for them. They used it religiously and just said that Max was the type of guy who liked pink. *"It works for him," Christine had said for a laugh.*

The laughter cleared the air for a moment. Audrey finally dared herself to ask: "Zach, how are you?"

Zach released his hands from his pockets. They hung sadly at his sides. "I am okay, I guess."

Audrey nodded. When he let the silence fall again, she pushed him a bit. "You um. You up to much?"

Zach laughed, but not unkindly. "Not so much. I guess that's obvious, given what I'm wearing and the state of my face." He pulled at his beard as if he was nervous once again.

Audrey's heart dropped a bit. "I really thought you'd left the island for good."

"I thought about it. I really did," Zach confessed. "And I

still am, I guess. I don't know how I can stay here with you now. After everything."

"Where did you go?"

Zach dropped his chin lower. "I went to visit my ex and our daughter's grave. I couldn't get the whole thing out of my mind. I had all these crazy flashbacks. I would wake up in the middle of the night and really think it had all just happened. My ex encouraged me to come back and get a therapist, which I've done now. The doctor says it's going to be a hard road, but I started medication and well." He shrugged again. "I guess that's my story and here I am on my daily mental health walk."

Audrey wanted to burst into tears. She knew, with every wrinkle etched into his face and every syllable, that he meant his words completely.

"Do you want to hold him?" she finally asked.

Zach looked at her like she had three heads. "Really? Are you sure?"

Slowly, Audrey lifted him from the stroller and placed him in Zach's arms. Their eyes connected as they assessed one another. The baby lifted a fist and pushed it against the top of Zach's chest, then kicked his feet excitedly. It was like a greeting between rowdy guys.

"Wow," Zach breathed. "He really is perfect."

"He's getting stronger by the day," Audrey said softly. "He's good. He's healthy. He has so much love for all of us. And although I know there are a million reasons to be afraid, I'm just trying to take one day at a time."

"One day at a time," Zach echoed. "What a concept."

Zach held baby Max another minute or so, more like he wanted to steal enough time to make up for never doing it again. With every move and sound he made, it was clear that he had been a father before. He knew what he was doing, despite the serious depression— despite the fact that he was basically a walking zombie.

When Zach placed Max back in the stroller, his eyes sparkled with tears. He straightened his spine and then said, "Christine made it pretty clear that she never wants to talk to me again."

Audrey had no idea how to respond. Her mind raced.

"But I'm glad I got to meet Max before he gets any bigger," Zach said. "Maybe I'll get off this island. Go build a life somewhere else. I don't know. But Audrey?"

"Yes?"

He pressed his lips together as he built the strength to speak again.

"I've been so privileged to be a part of your family the past year or so. All those weddings and birthdays and family dinners. All those nights beneath the stars. Throughout it all, I couldn't believe that I was allowed to be part of the Sheridan family. Now, I'm just grateful it ever happened."

They said goodbye after that. Audrey turned around to watch as he walked away. His posture was almost slouched in defeat, his head was low, and his hands were pushed in his sweatshirt again. He had none of the original Zach Walters swagger or confidence.

Audrey felt the tremendous weight of this meeting on her shoulders. But before she could think of what to do, Max started crying, and she lifted him against her chest, her hand cupping his perfect little head. Out across the waves, a tiny sailboat reflected the springtime sunlight. Maybe everything was just as lost as Zach said.

But then again, maybe not.

Chapter Nineteen

Max's check-up several days later was a barrage of good news. Max's oxygen levels were normal; he was growing healthily; and he seemed "just about the happiest baby," especially given what he'd gone through, according to the doctor. Christine and Audrey hugged outside the office as Max kicked around in his stroller. When Audrey stepped back, tears filled her eyes. "I just feel so relieved," she said. "I don't know why I expected bad news."

Christine laughed as she wiped a tear from her own cheek. "I think we just got used to bad news."

"That was our first mistake," Audrey said. "We should never let ourselves think that's the norm."

At this moment, Audrey again considered her run-in with Zach. She hadn't managed to explain the situation to Christine yet. Was this possibly the time? She didn't want to keep it from her.

Suddenly quiet, Audrey began to push the stroller out toward the sunny sidewalk. She didn't bother to zip up her spring jacket, and it whipped out behind her with the April breeze.

"Should we head to the grocery store?" Christine asked. "Amanda sent over one of her long lists."

"Of course she did," Audrey said. "Do you think she and Sam have kissed yet?"

Christine laughed heartily. "What a question! I don't know. They're certainly very chummy, aren't they?"

"I think she's smitten," Audrey added. "But she doesn't trust herself."

"Sam's a great guy," Christine affirmed. "Much better than that jackass, Chris."

"I checked Chris's social media recently," Audrey said, in full-on gossip mode. "He's in Thailand now, apparently. Having the time of his life. Scuba diving and riding motorcycles around islands."

"None of that sounds like anything Amanda would be into," Christine said.

"Wait. Imagine Amanda on the back of a motorcycle!"

"She would just scream the entire time," Christine returned.

"Audrey! Hey! Audrey?"

Audrey stopped short and drew her head around to spot Noah. He rushed across the parking lot, his dark locks swirling behind him in the breeze. When he reached the sidewalk, he gasped for air and said, "I saw you from all the way by the docks."

"That's quite a sprint," Audrey said with a laugh. Her heart jumped into her throat.

Noah studied her for a moment as his smile widened. There was real chemistry between them; Audrey couldn't deny it.

"It's Max's one-month birthday," she said suddenly.

Noah beamed down at Max. "I guess congratulations are in order, dude. You made it. One whole month on earth."

Audrey giggled as she slipped a strand of hair behind her ear. She could feel Christine's eyes boring into her head. Obviously, she'd turned into a flirtatious-college-student all over again.

Then again, seeing Noah like this was strange, as they'd been through so much together. They'd been through an emotional marathon.

"How is your sister?" Audrey asked.

"She's much better," Noah said. "Back home and everything. Mom couldn't be happier. She orders me around constantly. Everything we do is for the baby."

"Sounds like our house," Audrey said. "Max is the most spoiled baby on the planet."

"As he should be," Noah replied. After a pause, he added, "And I guess you're probably always at home with him, huh?"

What the heck did that mean?

"Mostly, I guess," Audrey said.

"Although we give each other breaks every once in a while. Don't we, Aud?" Christine chimed in.

Audrey turned to catch Christine's wink. *What did that mean? Was she playing cupid?*

"Oh, cool. So you could maybe, I don't know, go for a walk with me sometime?" Noah asked then.

Audrey's heart nearly burst out of her chest. Her first thoughts went to her bulgy belly, her tired eyes, and her frantic motherly thoughts. *Could she possibly leave the house for a few hours without Max? He was just a little thing.*

Then again, Christine would take over full-time as his guardian within the next few months.

She had to learn to give her the reins soon.

"I guess so. Yeah," Audrey heard herself say.

It was decided that they would meet in two nights' time

along the dock. They said goodbye and "see you later," and Audrey immediately entered a state of panic, one that reminded her of long-ago days when she'd actually known how to flirt with boys.

Once inside the grocery store, Christine was the first to speak. "The guy is in love with you."

Audrey's cheeks burned. She reached for a bag of apples, one of the items on Amanda's list, and placed it gently in the cart. "I don't know. We just hung out quite a bit when his sister and Max were in the NICU. Maybe he just wants a friend who understands what that was like."

"I've never looked at my friends like I want to undress them immediately," Christine teased. "Well, actually, that's not fully true. I'm sure there were a few guy friends over the years I wanted something more with."

"And didn't you and Zach kind of start out as friends?"

Christine stopped dead in her tracks near the oranges. Her face twitched. "Naw. More enemies, I guess. I should have known all along that it wouldn't have worked."

Audrey willed herself to explain that she had seen him. But she didn't want to hurt Christine any more than was necessary. Christine was broken-hearted; she just wanted to get through this pain and find a way to heal. Run-ins with Zach weren't going to help that.

* * *

Two days later, Max slept in his crib as Audrey hovered over her bed, where she'd splayed four potential outfits for her not-date with Noah. She'd hardly bothered with anything but sweats since Max's birth, and she wasn't entirely sure what her body would do with things like high-waisted jeans or cute black dresses. She began the grueling process of making the decision — buttoning what could be buttoned, yanking fabric over her shoulders, and frowning at her reflection in the mirror. Baby Max cooed at her throughout.

"It's all your fault, you know," she told him with a smile. "I used to be hot."

When she realized that not a single thing would do, she called her mother, on the verge of tears.

"I'll come and pick you up," Lola affirmed. "We'll figure something out."

Audrey hadn't spent much time at Lola's cabin, which she shared with Tommy. In recent months, she had redecorated the place to suit her personality. Prior to that, the place had just been drab and dark, too much of a reminder of the previous owner, Chuck, Scott's brother, who now sat in prison for stealing funds from many island residents.

"It's just like old times," Lola said. "You, raiding my closet."

Audrey laughed at the thought as she spread apart the various patterned fabrics, the black dresses, and the bohemian looks that her mother had accumulated over the years. Lola was something of a shopping addict, but she normally procured her goods from second-hand shops, so it all had this edge of "cool-ness" to it. You couldn't just go out and find it in any given store. Audrey's things were similar; they just didn't currently fit.

"You'd look so good in this," Lola said. She gripped a dark maroon full-length dress cut low across the breasts. "And your boobs are huge right now, so it's perfect."

Audrey rolled her eyes at the boob comment but took the dress and tried it on in the corner of the room. Although she'd changed in front of her mother countless times over the years, there was still something about her post-pregnancy body that she didn't want anyone to see.

When she turned back, she drew her shoulders back and lifted her chin.

"Wow. It really is beautiful," Lola remarked softly. "He won't be able to take his eyes off of you."

"Ugh. Whatever," Audrey said sheepishly.

In truth, though, when Audrey stood out by the docks in the dress, along with her mother's chic blue jean jacket, she really did feel like something special. It was maybe the first time since she'd gotten really huge that she felt pretty in any sense of the word. She glanced to the right and caught sight of Noah, walking toward her, his chin lifted and his smile big. Her heart flipped over in her chest.

Thankfully, her voice didn't give her nerves away.

"Hey there, stranger," she greeted with a smile.

Noah's eyes did a once over. "You look great," he said.

"So do you," she told him. And he did. Beneath his jacket, he wore a dark blue sweater and a pair of jeans. She could have burrowed herself against that sweater. She wondered what it felt like to have his strong arms wrapped around her.

They began to walk. The sun still hovered above the waterline, and everything was glossy with orange and pink light. Audrey was nervous at first and asked him silly questions, like what the personality of his baby sister was and what his mother's pregnancy cravings had been.

"She loved French fries," he said. "I was always running out to buy French fries. Oh, and dill pickles. She couldn't get enough."

"That's funny. I had a big thing for Fig Newtons," Audrey confessed. "We eventually had to ban them from the house."

Slowly, they eased the conversation toward other things. It felt natural, as though they were two flowers blooming along the branch of the same tree.

"Do you mind if I ask you a question?" Noah asked after about an hour. He leaned against a barrier between them and the water just beyond.

"Okay." For whatever reason, Audrey felt he could ask her anything at all. She wanted to be honest with him.

"The father," Noah started. "Max's dad. What happened there?"

Audrey didn't bristle against the question. "I was in Chicago for an internship. He was older. It was just a fling— an accident."

Noah nodded. "Do you think about him?"

Audrey shook her head. "I thought I would, but I don't. I have too much support from my family. And I don't even have to give up on my original plans. I'll be heading back to college soon to get my degree. And we get the added benefit of knowing and loving Max."

There was silence as Noah pondered what she'd said.

"Probably, it sounds crazy," Audrey said. "And honestly, it was. I was pregnant at nineteen. I was so disappointed in myself. I walked around with all this guilt. From the outside, I looked happy. I made jokes, and I laughed. But it was a year of a lot of pain for me. I felt like a prisoner in a lot of ways."

"I think I understand that," Noah said. "Although I can't fully imagine what it was like."

As their night continued, Audrey realized that this was the first time in a long, long time that she'd hung out with someone who wasn't directly linked to the Sheridan family. Date or no date, it was miraculous to be seen as Audrey— only Audrey, and not an extension of the Sheridans.

They grabbed ice cream, despite the chill of the late-evening air, and sat outside watching the boats bob against each other.

"I've thought about leaving in the fall," he said. "Heading off to school. I've done a few semesters, but I never fully committed to anything."

Audrey's throat tightened. She didn't dare dream any kind of dream.

"I'm just glad I could be here while my mom went through all this. And now that she has the baby to care for and love, I think she'll be okay if I left for a while." Noah paused and adjusted his ice cream cone. His eyes caught the last sight of the sunset. "Not that I don't miss this island when I'm gone. The Vineyard is in my blood. I don't think I'll ever live anywhere else long-term."

Audrey smiled. "I know exactly what you mean."

Chapter Twenty

It was a five-tiered, strawberry-cream-filled, flower-covered birthday cake. It was one of Christine's best creations, even better than the cake that had taken first prize at a competition in Paris, and she'd made it for Audrey's twentieth birthday celebration. It was an act of love and artistry. Of course, she'd seen Audrey wolf down three packaged pastry snacks in a row and mutter, "Wow, these are delicious," so she wasn't exactly the kind to be really impressed with fine cakes. That was okay.

When Christine delivered the cake to the Sheridan house, she found Amanda and Sam at the kitchen table, a bowl of mixed nuts and a bottle of wine between them. Baby Max slept in his bassinet in the corner, his eyelids glowing with their translucency. Amanda was so captivated by whatever Sam said that she hardly glanced up when Christine entered with the monster-sized cake.

"Wow. Christine!" Sam jumped up to assist her in placing the cake on the table. "You've outdone yourself."

"I think I got a little carried away," Christine admitted as she removed the cake cover. "And all this is for our birthday girl who normally eats cake with her hands."

"It's true. She does," Amanda affirmed with a laugh. "Or did. Maybe now that she's twenty, she'll outgrow it."

"I don't think Audrey will ever outgrow her Audrey-ness," Christine said. "And the world is better off for it." She removed her jacket and splayed it across one of the chairs. "Where is that girl, anyway?"

"She mentioned something about meeting a friend really quick?" Amanda said. Her eyes sparkled. "I have a hunch it's that guy. Noah."

"She's been so hush-hush about him since they went on that date last week," Christine said.

"She always corrects us and says it wasn't a date," Amanda explained to Sam.

This was ironic, Christine thought, since usually, when Amanda spoke about Sam, she always explained that they, too, "weren't dating." Oh, another generation of Sheridan women, up to their silly romantic tricks.

"I'm glad she's been allowed a little bit of fun," Christine said. "She almost went stir-crazy this past winter being pregnant and stuck inside."

"Pregnant and what?" Audrey's voice rang out from the back door. She appeared a few minutes later, her smile enormous and her hair all wild from the spring breeze from the Vineyard Sound.

"There she is! The birthday girl!" Christine said. She hugged Audrey close as Audrey exclaimed over the cake.

"You did not have to do this," she gushed as she inspected the masterpiece. "Oh my gosh! Those little flowers! How can I possibly eat them?"

"I think you can get yourself to eat anything," Christine replied with a laugh. "It's one of your superpowers."

Max got a bit fussy then, and Audrey took him upstairs to

feed him and change his diaper. Susan and Lola arrived with big bags of groceries. They seemed in the middle of an argument, which Christine only caught the tail-end of.

"I don't think you understand what I mean," Lola said. "Obviously, her lyrics are more poetic. I just don't think they're as musical."

"What the heck do you even mean?" Susan demanded.

Ah yes. Another silly sister argument. Maybe this was another sign of normality. They could go back to picking fights about stupid things.

Lola piled the grocery bags on the counter as Susan greeted Amanda and Sam.

"Don't mind us. We got heated in the car about nineties music, but I think we'll be over it soon," Susan explained with a playful grin.

"Speak for yourself," Lola grumbled.

"Good to see you, Sam!" Susan said. "Is Natalie working the front desk today?"

"Yep. I hope you don't mind that we switched shifts. I was invited to Audrey's birthday party," Sam said.

"Of course not," Susan said. "Glad to have you. We'll have enough food to feed a small country."

Amanda and Sam poured Susan, Christine, and Lola glasses of wine, as it was suggested that their "set-up party" would be more fun with a bit of tipsiness. Susan put on some nineties tunes to prove her point to Lola, and, although she was annoyed, Lola soon started to sing all the lyrics, as though she'd written them herself.

Audrey reappeared downstairs with the baby monitor. "I just want to let him sleep," she said. Her eyes glittered with excitement.

"He'll let us know when he needs us," Susan said as she placed a bouquet of flowers in a vase at the center of the table.

"He probably knows it's his mommy's birthday and doesn't want to ruin it for her."

"Ha. If he's anything like me, he's way too selfish for something like that," Audrey joked.

The party began a full hour before its scheduled time. People just couldn't resist popping by early. Kelli carried in mounds of snacks; Aunt Kerry brought a massive tray of potato salad; Beth had made about a thousand cookies; Charlotte brought a huge CorningWare dish of lasagna; and Scott, yet again, cranked up the grill to cook burgers and bratwursts and other BBQ delights.

As guests began to arrive, Audrey hustled upstairs and then reappeared in a beautiful dress, which she'd apparently borrowed from Lola. Lola planted a kiss on her daughter's forehead as she said, "I never should have given you a key to the cabin. You just come in and raid my closet whenever you please, now, don't you?"

"What are you talking about?" Audrey asked with a sneaky smile. "I've had this dress for years."

Christine hovered near the cake with a glass of wine. Several family members approached to compliment her on the cake. She couldn't help but sense that everyone spoke to her as though she was breakable; like, if they said something too jagged or too loud, she might break into a million pieces. Everyone had heard of the breakup; everyone felt awful. Susan had already interviewed a few candidates for the chef at the bistro, and she said all were promising. Time had moved on without old Christine. That was okay. Maybe.

Audrey found her about an hour later. She carried a paper plate, on which sat two blackened hot dogs, a mound of ketchup, and a massive brownie.

"That is quite an adult meal you have there," Christine said with a laugh.

"The dinner of a twenty-year-old," Audrey remarked.

"So. How was it earlier?" Christine asked. She grabbed Audrey's brownie, broke it in half, and ate a bit of the stolen chocolate morsel.

"How was what earlier?" Audrey asked. "And nobody told you that you could steal from the birthday girl."

"There are about four thousand more brownies on that table. I think you'll survive."

"Whatever. But what do you mean? How was what earlier?" Audrey asked.

Christine shrugged. "You know. When you left earlier. You met up with Noah, didn't you?"

Audrey's cheeks brightened to crimson. Finally, she shifted her weight, turned her eyes back toward the far end of the house, and said, "I did see him for a little while. We got a donut at Frosted Delights and walked around."

"I can see it in your eyes," Christine said. "You've got a huge crush."

Audrey laughed softly. Then, she added, "But Noah wasn't the only person I saw today."

"Oh?" Christine couldn't fully read Audrey's expression.

"I don't want you to be mad."

"Why would I be mad?" Christine asked.

"No reason," Audrey said with a light shrug.

At that moment, Amanda waved for Audrey to come over to her and Sam. "I wanted to tell Sam about that movie we watched the other day. What was it called?"

Audrey excused herself without another explanation, which left Christine only with a thudding heart and a quarter of a brownie in her hand.

But it didn't take long for Christine to get her answer. At around seven, Zach Walters appeared in the doorway of the Sheridan house. He stood in a pair of khakis and a polo shirt, with his face clean-shaven and a serious wrinkle between his brows. His eyes scanned across the room until they finally found Christine's. While chaos and conversation continued between them, they held one another's gaze for a long, long time.

What the heck was he doing here?

How dare he do this, after everything?

Audrey weaved her way through the crowd to reach him. Zach then lifted a little present, wrapped in silver wrapping paper, and passed it to her. She thanked him and hugged him, then whispered something in his ear. Christine felt like she was having an out-of-body experience.

So, this was who Audrey had run off to find.

Audrey had gone behind Christine's back to speak to Zach.

As though Audrey "knew what was best" for Christine.

Christine bristled at the thought. She genuinely thought she might lose her mind.

Audrey turned away from Zach and found Christine's dark gaze. Her smile fell immediately. She pressed through the crowd, gripped Christine's elbow, then snaked her toward Amanda's bedroom. Once behind the closed door, Christine's volatility poured out of her.

"Audrey! What the hell were you thinking?"

Audrey was pale. She knew she'd gone too far.

"Christine, listen. Please. Just listen."

"I just don't know why you thought it was okay to go behind my back like this. Do you understand how much pain I've been in since he left me like that? Do you know how long it's going to take me to heal?"

Audrey bit her lower lip as she tried to think of what to say. "I understand. I know it's been awful for you. But Christine—"

"I know you're still young, Audrey. But there are some things in life you really can't get over, no matter how hard you try," Christine continued. She was on the verge of tears.

"I ran into him, Christine." Audrey crossed her arms over her chest and glared at her. She looked exactly like her mother when Lola got angry. There was a storm in her eyes. "I ran into him, and he was a mess. I mean a complete mess. But he's on the path to getting better, Christine, and he's mostly doing it because he wants to be better for you. Don't you get that?"

Christine bit hard on her lower lip. Audrey continued to glare at her. It was like a stand-off.

"You shouldn't have invited him," Christine said meekly.

"Just go talk to him!" Audrey blared. "I swear, you're impossible. If you don't at least talk to him, then I don't know. Maybe you are a lost cause, just like you think you are."

The words were hurtful, yet they reeked of truth. Immediately after she said them, Audrey dropped her chin to her chest, heaved a sigh, and said, "Oh my God. I'm so sorry for saying that." After a pause, she added, "I didn't get much sleep last night. I'm running on fumes."

"It's okay, Audrey."

"No. It's not. What Zach did to you is so, so wrong. I just— I can't help but feel like you should at least hear him out."

Christine's heart felt tugged in a lot of different directions. On the one hand, Zach didn't deserve a second chance. On the other, didn't everyone?

"I'll do it," she said softly. "But only because it's your birthday."

Chapter Twenty-One

A few minutes later, Christine stood in front of Zach at the side of Audrey's birthday party. When she looked into those big blue eyes, she forgot to breathe. She could sense everyone's gaze upon her; she could already guess the kind of gossip that would surround them if she did, indeed, follow Zach out of the house. But she'd promised Audrey she'd do this. She had to be brave.

"Hi," she finally said, just loud enough for only him to hear.

"Hi," he returned.

It was laughable how much there was to say between them. The word "hi" was the tip of the iceberg. But it was a start.

Zach gestured with his head back toward the door. Reticent, Christine followed behind him. Although he'd maybe lost a bit of weight in the previous month, the muscles in his back remained powerful, and she loved to watch them shift beneath the fabric of his shirt. At the door, they both retrieved their coats from the closet, just as they'd done together countless times. Still wordless, they appeared outside.

"It's spring," Christine said. It was the stupidest thing she could have said. She cursed herself.

"It is. I can't believe it," Zach returned. This, also, was stupid, Christine thought.

And with that, they continued to walk in silence. The driveway was packed with vehicles from their family and friends, and they weaved through them, at-times parting ways and then finding their way toward the road. Once out there, they stood by the mailbox. Each time Christine's eyes met his, her heart jumped.

"I don't know what to say to you," Christine finally said. She decided it was better to live in honesty. There wasn't time for anything else.

"I know," Zach returned. "And I don't even know how to start."

He led her toward his car. There, he opened the back door and removed a big bouquet of lilies. Christine's knees knocked together as he passed them over to her. She was so weak that she felt she could hardly carry the bouquet. She shifted against the side of the car for support and gazed at them. They were beautiful, these big, pink, tender petals.

"You always told me that none of your ex-boyfriends ever got you flowers," Zach said softly.

A lump formed in Christine's throat, and she still couldn't speak.

"Christine, I know I can't fix what I did. I freaked out. I remembered all my past trauma, and it came back like a monster— all that pain. I knew I couldn't be the backbone you needed, or for Audrey, or for the baby. And I dropped into the worst depression of my life, at least since the accident.

"When I came to and started to go to therapy and took medication, things started to clear up. I can see clearly; I can think clearly. But I still have trouble sleeping because I know what I did put a rift between us. And maybe I can never have you back. I wouldn't blame you.

"It's just that, Christine, I want to build a life with you. I've wanted everything we've ever talked about. Raising Max, adopting more babies, and having a big, funny, wonderful family. I still want that. And if there's anything, anything at all I can do to get you back so we can do that, please, let me know."

Christine swallowed the lump in her throat. Again, her heart threatened to jump out of her ribcage. The silence stretched between them.

Until finally, she found the strength to speak.

"I just don't know."

Zach's eyes glistened with tears. "I understand."

"You hurt me so, so badly," Christine said.

Zach nodded. "I know that. But I hurt myself much, much more."

Christine believed him. She had to.

From the doorway, Susan called Christine's name. "Hey! Christine! We're about to do the cake!"

Zach's smile was terribly sad. "I guess you're needed."

"We can continue to talk about this," Christine finally said.

"An ongoing discussion?" Zach asked.

Christine shrugged. "If there's anything this year has taught me, it's that nothing is black and white."

"Shades of gray."

"Plenty of nuances," Christine agreed.

They held one another's gaze until Lola's voice rang out across the driveway and through the trees.

"Christine! Are you out there somewhere?"

"I swear, those Sheridan girls. They're impatient, aren't they?" Zach said with a laugh.

"To be fair to them, I'm the only one allowed to cut the cake. And when they're hungry for something, they want it as soon as possible," Christine said.

She and Zach shared another tender laugh as she stepped back. "Thank you for the flowers," she added. "There are way too many of them."

"Never enough," Zach insisted. "Give Audrey my best on her birthday."

"I will," Christine said.

"And baby Max, of course," Zach said. "That kid has it lucky, doesn't he?"

"He sure does," Christine agreed.

Back inside, Christine, Susan, Lola, Amanda, and Audrey wrapped themselves together, arm over shoulder over arm, and led the entire family in "Happy Birthday." Throughout, Audrey's eyes glittered with tears. She then closed her eyes and blew out the twenty candles, which Christine had positioned across two of the center tiers of the massive cake. (Of course, before this, she'd already photographed the cake elaborately, as she planned to send it into a few contests. It was really some of her finest work.)

As she portioned out the cake onto little paper plates, Audrey sidled up next to her.

"How did it go?" she asked under her breath.

Christine arched her brow. "I guess you want me to say that it went beautifully and we're back together and I'm all happy and in love again?"

Audrey nodded. "Yep," she said sarcastically.

"Well, it won't be easy," Christine offered, even as a smile spread between her cheeks. "But I think I do want to try again. I think there's a lot of love there. And maybe it's not good to abandon it."

Chapter Twenty-Two

"Six weeks old, Max. How did you get so big, huh?" Audrey stood above the crib as Christine hustled in and out of the bedroom in a flurry of panic. "Your Auntie Christine is acting like a teenager, isn't she?" Audrey continued to say to Max. "She's totally in love, and she doesn't want to admit it. Look at her. She's changed her outfit four times!"

Max cooed playfully. His blue eyes flashed as Christine walked back into the room, splayed her arms out on either side, and said, "Okay. What about this dress?"

Audrey chuckled and fell back on the bed. "I told you. You look beautiful in everything you've tried on."

"But what about this one in particular? The longer length of the skirt? Is it too much?"

"It makes you look tall and regal, like a princess," Audrey told her. "He'll be scared of you."

Christine rolled her eyes, turned around, and assessed herself in the mirror. Her long hair flowed almost perfectly down her shoulders, and the dark green dress cut in a cool square over her breasts. It hugged her hips beautifully, then dropped all the way to her toes. She imagined herself walking toward him, tripping on the skirt, and falling flat on her face.

"Need I remind you that this is Zach we're talking about?" Audrey asked as she stepped up behind her. She placed her chin on Christine's shoulder and made eye contact in the mirror. "Zach Walters is a man who already loves you. Even if you arrived in a trash bag, he would tell you how beautiful you looked."

"Ha."

Christine waited like an anxious teenager before prom downstairs on the couch. Hilariously, her father sat across from her and flipped through the channels as though he needed to approve her date before she ran off. Audrey came in and out with the baby until Wes reached out and took Max from her and cradled him against his chest and shoulder. The baby fell asleep almost immediately.

Amanda bustled in and out also, from her bedroom. She explained she was in the middle of a brutal online test for one of her classes and that she required numerous snacks to get through it. Audrey and Christine watched her as she gathered up pretzels, chips, and chocolates, all things the Type-A Amanda tried to avoid on a daily basis.

"Don't look at me like that," Amanda said as she disappeared back into her bedroom.

Zach rang the doorbell a few minutes later. Audrey squeezed her elbow and whispered, "Good luck," as Max's eyes flipped open, and he let out a whimper.

"Goodbye, little Max," Christine said. She waved at him, and the motion made his whimper stop abruptly. He watched her as she headed back toward the mudroom.

She donned her trench coat and stepped out into the evening light, where Zach awaited her. He was dressed in a suit jacket and a pair of slacks; his hair was styled; he was clean-shaven and his cheeks weren't as hollow as they'd been even a few days before. Christine inhaled sharply. Every muscle in her body screamed: *this man is terribly handsome. Don't mess this up.*

"Good evening," Zach said.

"Hello," she murmured shyly.

Zach opened the car door for her like a proper gentleman. She sat in a place she'd once been so accustomed to, her hands folded on her lap. He had cleaned the car recently. None of the familiar coffee cups were in the drink holders, and there was no sign of trash.

Zach got in and started the engine.

"Where are we off to?" Christine asked him.

"That's a surprise," he replied. He flashed her a sly smile, then eased back down the driveway. They drove in silence. Christine couldn't, for the life of her, think of a single thing to say. Everything felt too heavy. Maybe she could bring up the weather? The approaching summer season? The fact that Max now smiled genuinely— at only six weeks?

A few minutes later, Zach pulled the car into the parking lot along the Sunrise Cove Inn. Christine arched an eyebrow at him, incredulous. He'd even parked in the same spot they'd always parked in when they had worked there, side-by-side.

"Why are we parking here?" she finally asked.

"You'll see, okay?" he said.

Christine and Zach walked wordlessly through the double-wide doors and into the bistro. Upon their entrance, Ronnie, the busboy-turned-server, greeted them. He wore black and white like a proper server at a fancy restaurant. It didn't look very comfortable on him, although he really tried not to show it.

"Good evening," he said, making his voice much deeper than it normally was.

Christine wanted to laugh, but she held it back. She knew this was all a part of the ruse.

"Do you have a reservation?" Ronnie asked.

"We do. It's under Walters. Table for two," Zach said.

"Right. Just this way, please."

Ronnie led them through the empty restaurant, toward the back table, with a perfect view out the bay window overlooking the Vineyard Sound. The table had been decorated immaculately, with a white table cloth, beautiful china plates, several different forks, knives, and spoons, along with flowers, in an ornate vase.

"I think that vase belonged to my mother," Christine said softly. The memory of it curled through the back of her mind.

"It very well could have," Zach said. "We found it here at the inn."

They sat across from one another as Ronnie lit the candle between them. He then explained the set menu for the night.

"Tonight, we start with an amuse-bouche of lotus root and tenderloin," Ronnie explained, his hands behind his back. "After that, we have potato gnocchi in gorgonzola sauce, followed by a roasted carrot and avocado salad."

Christine's eyes grew wide. She mouthed to Zach, "What the heck did you do?"

"After that, we'll have a main dish of pistachio-crusted halibut," Ronnie said. "Followed by a dessert of crème brûlée. The chef would like to state that he's simply not as good as some at crème brûlée production but that he did his best."

When Ronnie disappeared to collect the first plates, Christine brought her hands out to wrap around Zach's at the center of the table.

"You made all this food for us?"

"Of course. I slaved away the past few hours," Zach said. "But it was some of the first cooking I'd done in six weeks. It felt great to do it again. Hopefully, I haven't lost my touch."

"How could the great Zach Walters forget how to cook?"

"You should have seen me. Making sandwiches the past few weeks," he said as he grimaced. "It was a sad time."

"Never again," Christine said with assurance in her voice.

"No. Never."

Ronnie arrived with the amuse-bouche. They began to eat quickly, as they were just as addicted to good food as ever before. They poured red wine from one of the Italian bottles as their smiles grew wider. The conversation began to flow naturally along with the wine, and soon, Christine felt as though they hadn't missed a single day.

"Tell me about Max," Zach said as they dove into the potato gnocchi.

Christine pondered this for a moment. "It seems a little unfair to label any parts of his personality at six weeks old."

Zach laughed. "I guess that's true. He's still trying to figure himself out."

"But if I can say it simply, he's just so inquisitive and wonderful, just the happiest little baby you'll ever meet," Christine said. "I haven't been around babies very much, so it's been kind of an adjustment for me. But I really have welcomed it. Even when Audrey and I are awake at three in the morning and we can't get him to stop crying. Even then, I feel only love."

Zach nodded. In his eyes, Christine could see flashes of memory from his long-ago days of fatherhood. He toyed with the gnocchi on his plate with a fork and then said, "I really hope I can get to know him. Max, I mean."

"I think that's up to Max," Christine replied.

At that, Zach actually burst into laughter. "I guess you're right about that. We'll have to talk to him."

"Schedule a meeting maybe," Christine shrugged her shoulders, then let out a laugh.

"I'll have my people call his people," Zach chimed in.

Ah, here it was— the banter they'd always had, which Christine had missed more than anything.

They continued to eat and drink and laugh into the night. Multiple times, Christine's heart screamed with how much she still loved him. Other times, her mind demanded the answer to one question: *can you really trust this guy?* But as the night continued, she free-fell back into his arms, her love. How could she resist this? How could she not find forgiveness when they had so much love for one another?

When they finished their crème brûlée and the last of the wine, the conversation filtered off for a moment. Christine was a little tipsy, and the candlelight's soft glow across his face made him all the more handsome.

"Are you ready to go home?" he asked her quietly. "It's almost midnight."

"Which home?" she asked.

He tilted his head. The question hung between them. "Well, which home do you want to go to?"

Christine swallowed and leaned forward. All she wanted in this world was to kiss him. "Let's decide when we get to the car."

Christine and Zach thanked Ronnie profusely. Ronnie looked terribly tired and a bit frightened, as apparently, when he'd fired up the crème brûlée he'd almost lost a finger. As Christine and Zach headed back to the car, she slipped her fingers through his and said, "How much did you pay Ronnie to do all that tonight?"

Zach laughed. "A lot more than he's ever earned in one night."

"Good," Christine returned.

Outside, Christine pressed her hand against Zach's chest. She had him pinned against the car. His blue eyes caught the light of the moon.

"You have me trapped," he said.

"I know. I have you just where I want you," Christine said.

She kissed him tenderly. The rush of it fell over her chest and made her stomach flip. Her ears buzzed and rang.

When the kiss broke, Zach whispered, "So. Have you decided which home you want to go back to?"

Christine nodded her teeth over her lower lip. "I think you know exactly where I want to go."

It was strange and beautiful to be back at the house with Zach. He'd cleaned it immaculately, as though he had hoped beyond anything she would return with him. He opened another bottle of wine as Christine settled in on her favorite seat on the counter. How many nights had they spent just like this, talking endlessly and kissing till it was far too late?

"I'm so glad you're back," Zach whispered as he lifted his lips toward hers again. "This house wasn't the same without you."

Chapter Twenty-Three

Audrey splayed her diary across her lap and realized, with a funny jump in her gut, that she hadn't written much since before giving birth. Her mind had been completely in the here-and-now, and she'd known no other action except:

1. Try to sleep (and fail)
2. See Max in the NICU
3. Try not to cry
4. Cry anyway
5. Eat something (preferably not something sugary, although, let's be honest— that's normally what happens)
6. Repeat

Now that Max had been around for nearly two months, in good health and growing like a bean, Audrey had the strength to return her pen to the pages of her diary. She sat out on the porch swing, a blanket wrapped around her, with Max, all bundled up, in his carrier on the porch. Audrey had just checked on Grandpa Wes; he'd gone down for a nap and hadn't stirred in a few hours. There was something so peaceful about this sunny day. She imagined him lying on his bed and watching the sun play out through the lacey drapes.

Dear Diary,

It's now April 20.

Where the hell should I even begin?

Since Christine's reunion with Zach, she'd split her time between the Sheridan house and her place with Zach. It was decided that until Audrey returned to school, she'd keep the nursery things at the Sheridan house. Christine would spend some nights there to make sure that once the transition from Audrey to Christine and Zach happened, Max would be really accustomed to seeing Christine's face in the night. Christine liked the arrangement just fine. "It's like I get the best of both worlds," she'd said.

A spring breeze shifted beneath the porch swing. It creaked to-and-fro beneath her. She turned her eyes back toward Max, whose little fingers curled over the top of the blanket so tenderly that it made her heart break open.

Just past two in the afternoon, Audrey heard the back door-bell ring. She lifted the carrier with baby Max inside, slipped through the kitchen, and opened the screen door to find her expected visitors. Willa and Cassie had decided to come down for the day to meet baby Max and tell her all the news of Penn State's spring semester.

Willa and Cassie shrieked when they saw Audrey. Audrey placed a finger on her lips and said, "Shh! He's asleep!"

"Shoot," Cassie said as she clapped her hand over her mouth. "I kind of forgot. I'm sorry."

They looked beautiful, alive, and healthy. Audrey poured them each a glass of wine from her aunt's stash, and they sat out on the porch overlooking the water. Willa and Cassie both said all the right things as they doted on Max.

"He looks just like you," Cassie said.

"I think he looks like my grandfather," Audrey told her.

"But he's just so sweet! Don't you want to eat him?"

Audrey chuckled. "Sometimes."

The conversation turned to other things. Audrey was terribly curious about what had happened since she'd last seen them, and the girls had nothing but gossip to fill her in on. Willa had had a tumultuous affair with a grad student about five years her senior, and Cassie had done her very best to sleep with a professor but had ultimately failed.

"I really wanted that dramatic story," Cassie moaned.

"I know. But we have more semesters," Audrey said with a laugh. "I'm sure you'll find a professor who is open to destroying his life for you."

"Thank you for saying that. Willa hasn't been as supportive as you in all this," Cassie said.

"I just think there are a ton of perfectly good-looking guys, who are actually students, is all," Willa said.

Audrey fed them croissants, which they smeared with butter and ate heartily while complaining about carbs. This made Audrey giggle inwardly.

"It's going to be just like this, isn't it?" Willa asked. "The three of us, in our next place? Sure, we won't have the ocean. But we'll have all the gossip."

Audrey's heart felt squeezed when she considered it. How could she possibly leave Max?

But then again, it had been a part of the plan since the very beginning.

"Ah! Didn't you say you could sign up for your classes this afternoon?" Cassie asked suddenly.

Like other semesters, Audrey had been given a "time window" during which she was meant to get online and sign up for classes. She nodded, her eyes widening. "Do you want to help me?"

Somehow, she needed her girlfriends there with her to help her make the next step. Otherwise, she might get caught in the cycle of Martha's Vineyard, of motherhood, and allow this world that she'd grown to love to swallow her whole. She didn't want to regret not going to college, though. It wasn't even all for Max and how he saw her. In actuality, it was also for her. She needed to do it to prove something to herself.

Together, Audrey, Cassie, and Willa peered at the computer screen while Audrey selected a number of classes for her second year of college at Penn State. A number of them were journalism-related, while others were literature or creative writing. Unfortunately, she had to take a math class, but Willa said she'd taken the same one and had saved her notes. "You won't even have to go to class or anything," she said. "I kept everything."

Amanda walked in as they finished up the class schedule. She dropped her earphones from her ears and beamed at them there at the kitchen table.

"I didn't know you had guests!" she said.

"Sure do," Audrey said. "But where have you been all day?"

"Oh, I just helped Sam out with something at the inn," Amanda said.

Audrey arched an eyebrow. "Uh-huh." She then turned to Willa and whispered, "Amanda really likes to help Sam. A lot."

"Hush!" Amanda said, cackling as she sat with them and poured herself a glass of wine. "Sam's a good guy. And he's still pretty new to the island. I can't just let him float away."

"I see you want to have one of these for yourself," Audrey teased, gesturing toward Max, who continued to sleep, thankfully.

Amanda blushed. "Come on. Not yet. Plus, you know me. I just got out of a crazy long relationship. I just have to see what's out there."

"Yeah, girl. Go out there and see what you find!" Cassie said.

"I know you, Amanda Sheridan. You love *love* more than you love lists," Audrey added.

"Come on. As if people haven't seen you and Noah out for your little walks along the dock," Amanda said, taking a sip of her wine.

"Oh my God!" Willa cried. She snapped her head around to glare at Audrey. "Who. Is. Noah?"

Audrey gave Amanda a funny smile. "Thanks."

"Don't mention it," Amanda smirked playfully.

"Come on, Aud. Who is Noah?" Willa whined. "It's so like you to have a boyfriend the minute you give birth. All the boys were obsessed with you freshman year."

"And they were even more obsessed this year because they noticed you weren't with us!" Cassie cried. "It was so annoying. We'd roll up to a party, and the first thing we hear? Where's Audrey?"

Amanda crossed her arms over her chest. A small smile played at the edges of her mouth.

"You're really pleased with yourself, aren't you, Amanda?" Audrey asked. "But I'll have you know, me and Noah are just friends. He's trying to decide what to do after this. He might go to college, too."

"Wow. I wonder what school he's considering," Amanda said. "Has he maybe heard of ... Penn State?"

"Oh my God!" Willa and Cassie cried in unison.

Audrey rolled her eyes. Just then, her mother walked in through the back door, leading Aunt Susan, who carried two grocery bags. Lola had been out on the sailboat with Tommy all day, and her cheeks were sun-tinged.

"Girls! Hi!" Lola beamed. She dropped down to kiss both Willa and Cassie on the cheeks. "I'm so glad you're here."

"We just learned that Audrey is in love," Willa said.

Lola arched her brow. "We're all in love. As Sheridan

women, if we're not in love, then we're doing something wrong."

"Maybe we should get that embroidered on a pillow," Susan said from the kitchen.

Cassie and Willa stayed long into the night. Audrey loved watching them take turns with baby Max. They talked about what would happen later on when Christine and Max visited campus. "We have to show him everything!" Cassie cooed. "And we'll have to get him a school jersey."

"Definitely," Willa agreed.

It was a beautiful thing watching Audrey's two worlds come together. She was so grateful her dearest friends from far away had decided to include themselves in this fresh decision. It told her something about their character. It told her she should cling to them for as long as she could.

They set Cassie and Willa up in one of the bedrooms upstairs while Audrey stayed up with Max, who wouldn't stop crying. At various points through the night, she felt a pang of strange guilt about having arranged classes for herself for the following semester; at other points, she brimmed over with excitement.

As the baby calmed across her chest, Amanda appeared in the doorway in her pajamas.

"Hey you," Audrey said.

Amanda sat cross-legged across from her on the floor. "I'm sorry for giving you and Noah away."

"Don't worry about it." Audrey laughed softly. "Nothing has happened yet. Maybe it never will."

"I feel the same way about Sam," Amanda returned.

"But you know if you went for it, he would say yes, right?" Audrey said.

Amanda shrugged and splayed her hands across her cheeks. "I don't actually know that for sure."

"Well. You know what's coming, don't you?" Audrey offered.

"What do you mean?"

"Summer, Amanda. Summer's coming. On Martha's Vineyard, only magical things happen in the summer," Audrey said. "The island is about to come alive. And if there's any time for you and Sam to fall in real, serious, undying love— it's then."

Chapter Twenty-Four

April 24

Christine checked the calendar in the bistro kitchen as she scrubbed her hands. It was just past four in the morning, and she had about five loaves of bread, three-dozen cookies, several pies, and countless croissants to bake. She flicked on the radio and shuffled across the tile floor, yanking various bowls and spoons and mixers from their compartments. Here, she was in her element, but as of late, she'd really felt in her element everywhere. When she had cradled Max the previous night at the Sheridan house, he'd fallen asleep almost instantly. When she had spoken to Zach about something he did that bothered her a week before, he'd made immediate alterations. It was like everywhere she went, as long as she went there with confidence and love, the universe responded kindly.

It was definitely a weird feeling. Christine just wanted to appreciate it for all it was.

But as she turned the mixer over the flour, eggs, sugar, baking soda and vanilla mixture, something in her stomach shifted. She placed a hand over her mouth and sped off to the bathroom just off of the kitchen. She flung over the toilet and spewed as though she was drunk out of her mind at a club in Manhattan and not bright-eyed and bushy-tailed, at work on Martha's Vineyard.

What the hell?

Christine cleaned herself. Probably, she'd just eaten something off.

But when it happened the following day, and then the next, she began to worry. She didn't explain the situation to anyone, not yet, but she did go everywhere a bit slower, with a bit more apprehension. Susan had only just recovered from cancer; it was possible that there was something seriously wrong with Christine, too. She was now forty-three, after all. It wasn't outside the bounds of reason to say that her body might begin to break down on her.

Around April 27, Christine noticed that her breasts swelled and ached. The pain actually kept her up through the night. Zach rolled over around three, noticed she was still awake, and asked, "Are you okay? You're just frowning toward the ceiling."

Christine shifted beneath the blankets. "My boobs hurt."

Zach rubbed at his forehead. "What? That's weird, right?"

"Yeah. It's weird."

"Has it ever happened before?"

"Nope."

Christine knew as a darkness descended over her that Zach was thinking exactly what she was— that maybe she was sick the way Susan had been sick. Maybe, they had a whole other mountain to crawl up together.

"You should go to the doctor," Zach said. "If it's really bothering you."

Christine sniffed. "I don't think so."

There was silence for a long time. Finally, Zach said, "You aren't just going to get better by ignoring the problem."

"Maybe I will," she replied.

"It's never happened before," Zach said. "Not in the long history of modern medicine."

Still, over the next few days, as Christine went to work, baked bread, sat with her sisters, and watched Max, she felt a number of things and none of them were entirely good. She was frequently dizzy; her breasts ached; her mouth was dry, and she threw up almost every other day. She didn't mention any of it to her sisters, although once, Susan asked if she was okay.

"You look a little pale. Are you eating enough?" she'd asked.

"I'm fine. It's just been a lot of stress now that Zach's back at the bistro. We have such a packed schedule."

* * *

As it rolled into April 30th, Christine sat out on the back porch with Audrey, Susan, Lola, and Amanda. Max slept in his carrier toward the far end of the porch, with a beautiful view of the water. All the women had agreed that they wanted him to see as much of the Vineyard Sound as possible.

"I can see it. He already wants to get out there," Audrey said softly.

"Tommy can teach him the ropes," Lola declared.

Susan flipped through another wedding magazine as she explained to them what she'd already arranged for the upcoming June 19 ceremony, to be held at the Sunrise Cove.

"Charlotte has been exceptional in planning everything," Susan said.

"It's almost like she's one of the most famous wedding planners on the planet," Audrey said with a mischievous smile.

"Ha. True," Susan agreed.

"We just don't have a dress yet," Amanda said with a sigh.

"Next week, maybe," Susan said. "And the shoes."

"The shoes! Arguably the most important part of the whole ceremony," Lola said knowingly.

"Is Dad going to walk you down the aisle?" Christine asked.

Susan nodded. Her eyes grew misty. "He didn't get to do it the first time. It makes me so happy that he can do it now."

Christine and Lola made heavy eye contact after that. Both of their thoughts were lost on her last words. Maybe, just maybe, they'd both have the chance to have Wes walk them down the aisle, too. But they knew, with dementia, life was a ticking time bomb— always.

Suddenly, Christine jumped to her feet. She placed her hand over her mouth, then rushed through the door and hustled to the downstairs bathroom. Again, she retched into the toilet as shame overtook her. She hadn't wanted to show her sisters anything about this weird illness. Like Zach had said, she just wanted to hide from it all.

She hustled upstairs afterward, brushed her teeth, splashed water over her face, and gazed at herself for a long time. Whatever this was, she could handle it.

But before she could return downstairs, she spun around to find Audrey in the doorway of the upstairs bathroom. She blinked at her with big, wide eyes— without a single layer of sarcasm and said, "Do you think you're pregnant?"

Christine had not thought of this. Not even once. She furrowed her brow and scoffed.

"Um, no. I only have one ovary, remember?"

Audrey shrugged. "I don't think it's impossible."

"It's basically impossible. Trust me. I've read every single stat, and the doctor told me it would be one in a million."

"I've watched you run to the bathroom to throw up like three times this week," Audrey said.

Christine had no idea Audrey was paying such close attention. Her cheeks warmed with embarrassment.

"What does Zach think?" Audrey asked.

"About what?"

"About you being so sick?"

Christine was quiet for a moment. "He wants me to go to the doctor. He's worried."

Audrey chewed on her lower lip. "Do your boobs hurt?"

Christine's heart nearly stopped beating. "I mean, yes."

"Just promise me you'll take a pregnancy test before you rule it out, okay?" Audrey said.

"I told you. It's impossible."

"Just like it was impossible for you to forgive Zach?"

"This is quite a bit different. This is biology, not romance," Christine insisted.

* * *

But Audrey had gotten into her head. This was just like Audrey, to dig into the back alleys of her mind and claw her way in until Christine was forced to take notice. That night, as she drove back toward the house she shared with Zach, Christine stopped by the convenience store. After a deep breath, she forced herself inside.

Christine wandered the aisles for a long time before she made her way to the pregnancy tests. She analyzed almost every top story in various trash magazines, and she contemplated buying several different kinds of chocolate, which she'd started to crave with reckless abandon lately. She also thought about changing cleaning supplies for the house since whatever she now used had a smell that had just started to bother her.

Now that she considered it, from many angles, Audrey had a very valid point.

There was something very particular about this illness.

But she didn't dare hope.

She couldn't hope.

At the register, Christine placed four pregnancy tests on the counter. The girl who checked her out was maybe twenty years old. Christine wondered if the girl thought she was too old to be a mother.

But probably, the girl barely thought of her at all.

Back at home, Zach stood at the stovetop. He had the night off from the bistro, and he wore a pair of joggers that sat just above his hips and a black V-neck t-shirt. He looked chipper and happy, his eyes aglow, as he greeted Christine with a kiss.

"I'm making tacos for us. Homemade tortillas, obviously," he said.

"Obviously," Christine repeated. She tried to smile, but it fell off her face almost immediately.

She was so nervous. She could hardly stand up.

And in fact, as she made her way into the bathroom, she nearly toppled over as she tried to pee on the stick while sitting on top of the toilet. She placed the cap back on and waited with her underwear around her ankles. She didn't dare breathe. Two stripes meant pregnant. Just one meant not. All her life, through all of her "mistakes," she'd only had one stripe. Never. Pregnant. It had never been her time.

But as she stood there, her knees clacking together with shock and panic and hope, she watched incredulously as that second pink line formed alongside the other.

And in a moment, that second pink line was almost as strong and powerful as the first.

The next minute was a kind of a blur. Christine placed the lid on the toilet and curled up in a ball on top of it. She held the pregnancy test up in the air as though, at any moment, it might decide to change its mind.

How was this possible?

After all those years?

With only one ovary?

She and Zach hadn't been careful. But they'd never been careful, and it had never mattered before.

But here and now.

It was proof of something.

Her hand covered her mouth as a gasp escaped. She thought about the enormity of what this meant. She felt her tears roll down her cheeks a second later. Then, there was a knock at the door, but Christine couldn't bring herself to answer it. Finally, the door opened. Zach stood, worry etched between his eyebrows.

"Christine, what happened?" he asked softly. "What— what is that?"

Christine turned the pregnancy test around to show the two lines.

And at that moment, Zach fell to his knees. He looked up at her again and then wrapped Christine in the largest, warmest, most incredible hug. He tightened his grip until his cries made her shake, too. Together, they held each other— knowing another Sheridan baby was growing in Christine's belly. Christine had never imagined life could work in such mysterious ways. But she was so glad she'd been given a chance to see what would happen next.

Everything happened for a reason. She wasn't about to argue with any of it.

* * *

Next in the series

175

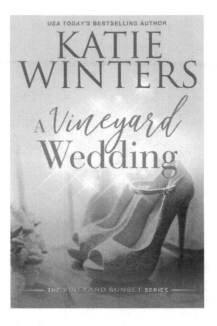

Other Books by Katie

Connect with Katie Winters

BookBub
Facebook
Newsletter

To receive exclusive updates from Katie Winters please sign up
to be on her Newsletter!
CLICK HERE TO SUBSCRIBE